CW00406450

Home to Me
The Andrades
Book Two

Ruth Cardello

Home To Me
The Andrades

Copyright © 2014 Ruth Cardello

First Printing, 2014, Paperback edition 1.0
ISBN: 978-1502495709

This book or any portion thereof may not be reproduced
or used in any manner whatsoever without the express
written permission of the copyright owner except for the
use of brief quotations in a book review.

This is a work of fiction. Any resemblance to actual
persons, places, event, business establishments or locales
is entirely coincidental.

Print cover by Trevino Creative

Author Contact
Website: RuthCardello.com
Email: Minouri@aol.com
Facebook: Author Ruth Cardello
Twitter: RuthieCardello

Dedication:

*To my husband, Tony, and my three amazing children.
No matter where we live, or how far we roam, you will always
be HOME TO ME.*

Chapter One

"YOU CAN'T STOP me—don't get hurt trying to," Nick Andrade warned as he moved to sidestep Rena, his brother's secretary, for a second time.

Her chest bounced beneath her thin silk blouse and her hands went angrily to her hips, momentarily distracting Nick. Rena had always been a twelve on his one-to-ten scale. He preferred blondes as a general rule, but she was his exception. "I'm not letting you by. Gio is on an important international call."

"I don't care."

"That's exactly why you're staying out here with me."

As she blocked him, daring him to test her resolve, he felt his blood rush downward and was reminded why she was trouble and always had been.

Too vividly, he recalled another day when a younger Rena had stood before him in almost exactly the same pose. Gio had just started working full-time at his family's oil company, Cogent, and he had asked Nick to pick up papers from his friend Kane. Nick had agreed even though it was a long drive. He'd only been home for a day and had already had a row with his mother, so any excuse to get out, even going to Sag Harbor, had been a welcome reprieve.

Rena had opened the door to her family's home dressed in shorts and T-shirt emblazoned with her college's name, taken one look at him, put her hands on her hips, and said, "Nick, I'm surprised you're still alive."

Her shirt had hugged her young breasts, and the long expanse of thigh exposed by her shorts had temporarily wiped all sense from his head. Yep, trouble. She was Kane's little sister—even called herself an honorary Andrade because of all the time she'd spent with them while growing up.

Practically part of the family.

Forbidden.

"Rena, a pleasure to see you, as always. Gio asked me to pick up a folder."

Rena had nodded. "Kane said he left something in the den in case you came by. Would you like to come in?"

He'd shaken his head. He'd never liked being at the Sander's house. Gio had spent most of his vacations there, but Nick would rather have had needles stuck beneath his fingernails than spend five minutes with Rena's parents. They were always smiling, always asking about things that were none of their business, and offering advice when it was clearly not requested or welcome.

Gio had claimed they did it because they cared. Nick had seen it as a genetic defect, and one they had passed down to their children.

"I'll wait here," Nick had answered and leaned against the doorjamb.

"Suit yourself," she'd said and walked back into the house. When she'd returned she'd held up the folder but hadn't immediately handed it over to him. "Gio was upset when he saw the photos of you and your friends jumping out of that helicopter to ski in Vail."

"Everything upsets Gio..."

"He worries about you. He thinks you're going to get yourself killed with one of your stunts. I think so, too."

Nick had snatched the folder easily out of Rena's hand. "It's called having fun, Rena. You should try it sometime. Oh, wait, Mommy and Daddy would never give you permission, would they?"

"My parents would support whatever I wanted to do."

With a whistle, Nick had mocked her. "Then come to Martha's Vineyard with me this weekend. I just got my pilot's license. I'm flying a bunch of friends up to our beach house. Even Stephan is coming. It's going to be wild."

"I can't. I have finals next week."

"I'm sure you could blow off studying this one time and still pass your classes."

"I probably could, but I'm not going to."

"Why bother when a job will be handed to you as soon as you graduate?"

"My grades are important to me."

"You mean, they're important to your parents."

"That too. I don't like disappointing them."

"My God, you sound like you're twelve."

Rena's face had reddened and she'd spat, "Fuck you."

He's tossed her a lopsided grin. "Thanks for the offer, but I don't do virgins."

"You're such an asshole, Nick."

Nick had waved the folder, chuckled, and said, "It's what the ladies love about me."

Rena had turned and slammed the door in a glorious huff, leaving Nick standing outside, shaking his head in bemusement. He loved the wild look in her eyes when her temper flared, and that he was the only one who could make her that angry. She was innocence and fire, and he'd spent many nights wanting to intimately explore both sides of her.

He'd never pursued her, though. She'd started working for Gio after college, and he'd promised his brother he'd stay away from her. He couldn't forget her, though, as hard as he tried. Shit, she even sent him a card for his birthday every year.

Lately it was the only one he received. He'd never thanked her for any of them. Honestly, he half hoped each year would be the last year he'd get one, but they kept coming. They made him angry for reasons he couldn't fully understand. Who the hell takes the time to remember an adult's birthday?

She'd taken the "nice girl next door" act too far. All her boyfriends were educated, well dressed, and boring as hell. She was, too, when she was with them. He'd bet none of them knew Rena was a sucker for a dare, or that she ate before she went out because she wanted to appear satisfied by a salad.

They might not know her quirks, but they'd experienced something he hadn't—the taste of those lips. They knew the way she moaned when she was just about to come. With his heart beating wildly in his chest and adrenaline rushing through his veins, Nick allowed himself the luxury of imagining how she would look in his bed after hours of being fucked.

He met her eyes and came crashing back to the present. *What the hell am I doing?* He'd come to confront his brother, and doing so while sporting a hard-on was not in his plans. "Gio needs to hear what I have to say. It's a hell of a lot more important than whatever he's doing, which I'm sure is promising to blow whoever's on that call to land his latest deal."

"Are you drunk?" Rena asked, her forehead creasing with concern.

"No," he said impatiently. *Just an idiot who needs to ignore how tightly your skirt is hugging your beautiful ass.*

She leaned in and sniffed. He knew that concerned look well. He could have told her he'd stopped drinking completely when he'd returned from his cousin's wedding, but he didn't explain himself to anyone. "Get out of my way."

Her chin raised a notch and her eyes narrowed. "No."

Nick had never touched a woman out of anger, and he never would. Still, her show of loyalty to his brother fueled his anger. He knew one method that would get her to retreat and he wasn't above using it. He gave her a blatant, appreciative once-over and wiggled his eyebrows suggestively. "I can think of something that would stop me."

She flipped her hair over one shoulder and shook her head. "You're trying to make me angry."

Nick stepped closer to her. "Anger isn't what I'd make you feel." He ran a finger lightly down her tense jaw and over the wild pulse in her neck. Instead of turning tail and running, she held his eyes, and Nick inhaled harshly. The air between them throbbed with a desire that neither would admit to. Her eyes dilated, and her lips parted just enough that he could imagine slipping his tongue between them and tasting her.

She bit her lower lip gently between her teeth. He groaned audibly and stepped closer, his mouth hovering above hers. For no more than a heartbeat or two, he forgot why he'd initiated this exchange. He was just a man who was about to kiss a woman he wanted, one he'd denied himself for as long as he could remember.

The door behind her flew open. "What are you doing here, Nick?"

Rena's eyes searched his in confusion. Then she looked away, a slight blush spreading across her cheeks. Nick raised his head and squared his shoulders. "We need to talk, Gio."

Rena addressed Gio. "Should I call Luke?"

"No," Gio said in an irritatingly authoritative tone.

"Wise choice," Nick said over Rena's head. "You won't want him to hear what I have to say."

Gio raised one mocking eyebrow, then motioned for Nick to come into his office. Anger rushed through Nick. *He doesn't take me seriously. He never has. That is about to change.*

Rena put a hand on Nick's arm when he moved to step around her. The light touch was fire on his skin, painful and pleasurable at the same time. In a volume so low only he would hear her words, she said, "Whatever happened, don't let it come between you. You're family. There is nothing more important than that."

"You don't know what this is about."

"No, but I know Gio."

"Your concern for him is touching." Nick stepped away from her and through the door his brother held open for him.

Just before the door closed, he thought he heard Rena whisper, "It's not him I'm worried about."

CB

Rena Sander paced the carpeted floor in front of her desk. Nick Andrade knew exactly how to get her blood boiling. Yes, she found him attractive, but a woman would have to be dead not to. The Andrade men had all been blessed with good looks. Each had eyes as dark as coal and strong features that would have done any Roman statue proud. Well over six feet with a naturally muscular build, and consistently dressed in casual but expensive international designer clothing, Nick always looked like he'd just finished a cover shoot for *GQ*.

He used his good looks to get what he wanted, and today that had meant getting around her. How far would he have gone to achieve his goal? And would his ploy have worked? Rena was glad she'd never know. Whatever feelings she'd once had for him were in the past. As she'd grown up, they'd fallen by the wayside, as all teenage crushes should.

Now was not the time to start asking what-ifs.

Plus, dating Nick was probably the only way she could lose her job at Cogent, and she didn't want to. It wasn't a perfect job. Gio had a reputation for being demanding, impatient, and often blunt when a softer touch was warranted, but Rena wasn't bothered by his moods. He'd even fired her a few times since she'd started there. She hadn't taken him seriously, and he'd always called back to apologize and rehire her.

Job security was a perk of being his best friend's little sister, but she worked hard to make sure she deserved to be there. No one worked longer hours or was more dedicated to the company than she was, and she was proud of how she could keep the office functioning seamlessly during Gio's many business trips.

Kane teased her that she only wanted to work there because it kept her in the middle of any and all Andrade drama. Rena would have denied it, but she didn't like to lie. Gio and his brothers needed her. *When someone needs you, you help them—whether or not they ask you to.*

It's practically our family motto.

Permission to assist appreciated, but not necessary.

Over the eighteen or so years she'd known them, she'd watched the four Andrade brothers grow from sad boys into angry men. They each hid their scars in different ways, but they didn't fool Rena. Yes, they had lived a privileged life that, on the surface, appeared ideal, but Rena knew the truth of how they'd been raised. Between their workaholic father and their viciously insecure and spiteful mother, they'd been deprived of what Rena considered any semblance of a healthy home. They craved love and understanding like half-wilted flowers crave water.

Gio: the angry family patriarch. His word was law and his temper was short. Until he met his fiancée, Julia, he'd hidden himself away in his work. The change in him had been heartwarming. More than ever before, it made Rena wish the same happiness for the others.

Nick: the unredeemable and notorious playboy. Young, rich, and gorgeous. He was photographed more than many movie stars were, and could be counted on to consistently provide front-page-worthy scandalous photos. His dating practices were legendary—heiresses to porn stars—and if half of what the papers claimed he'd done were true, he'd have a lot of explaining to do if he ever made it to the gates of Heaven.

Luke: the rich surgeon and the glue of the Andrade family. He called his brothers daily and smoothed over whatever was brewing. He reminded her of her brother, Kane.

And Max: the youngest, who had branched off to make his own fortune in the hotel and casino business. He was the most private of the four boys and the one Rena knew the least. In general, he kept himself outside of all family drama.

Rena reached for the phone and called the brother she'd been told not to. "Luke?"

"Rena," Luke answered warmly. "I'm about to go into surgery. Can we talk later?"

"Nick is here," Rena said in a rush.

"That's good. I've talked to him about getting more involved at Cogent. I'm glad he's doing it."

Rena began pacing again with the headset in her hand. "I don't believe his visit is business related. Nick said he had something he needed to say to Gio and he didn't look happy about it."

"Shit." Luke sighed. "I can't come now. Do you have any idea what it's about?"

"I was hoping you did."

"Nick has been spending time with our mother since she had that episode."

"You mean her heart attack?"

"I haven't seen her health records, so I can't say for sure. It might have been a severe panic attack."

"You think she lied?"

Luke sighed again. "No. She wouldn't go that far, but she could exaggerate the situation. She hasn't been the same since we attended Stephan's wedding without her. I don't know what she has against Victor and Alessandro, but she can't handle the idea of any of us spending time with either of them. I've tried to talk to her about it, but she won't discuss it."

"So you think she said something to Nick?"

"I don't know. She's upset that Gio isn't speaking to her right now. Maybe it's about that."

"They had an argument right after the wedding, didn't they?"

"That's what I hear. Gio was furious with her for trying to pay off Julia."

"I still don't understand why she would do that. Julia makes Gio happy. Who wouldn't want her son to find love?"

"She would tell you she does whatever is necessary to protect us. For some reason that included keeping Julia and Gio apart."

"I don't think Patrice likes you and your brothers getting along the way you have since Stephan's wedding. I wouldn't put it past her to have faked an *episode* just to draw attention back to herself."

"Hey," Luke reprimanded.

"Sorry, I know she's your mother. I just don't understand her. She has four amazing sons and more money than she could spend in ten lifetimes. Why isn't she happy?"

"I wish I knew," Luke said sadly. "She's heading to a dark place. I hope she doesn't take Nick with her."

Rena stopped and chewed her lip. "I could talk to him."

"Listen, I know you care. I wouldn't tell you this if I didn't consider you one of us, but don't get involved this time. I have a feeling this is going to get really ugly before it gets better. I don't want to see you get hurt."

Rena laughed even though she found little humor in the situation. "You're the second Andrade to say that to me today. Nick said almost those exact words a few minutes ago. You should have seen his face when he said it. Something really upset him today. I wish I knew what it was."

"Don't do it, Rena."

"What?"

"Don't try to help Nick. He's right. You'll only get hurt."

"I wish the four of you could always be as happy as you looked right after you came back from the island wedding."

With a sigh, Luke said, "I have to go. Rena, promise me you'll let them sort this out themselves. I have some time late this afternoon. I'll come by to smooth over whatever blowup they have this morning. Stay out of it."

"I will."

"You're not a good liar, Rena."

Rena hung up the phone and squared her shoulders. *Maybe not, but if Nick and Gio wanted me to stay out of this, they would have had their spat away from the office.*

Rena placed her hand on the door to Gio's office and took a deep breath.

I will not stand back and do nothing while they tear each other apart.

Sorry, Patrice. Whatever you're up to is not going to work. Not this time.

Not on my watch.

Chapter Two

"I WENT TO see Mother this morning," Nick said slowly, watching his brother's reaction. Of his three brothers, Gio was the most difficult to talk to about anything. Luke could always be relied on to provide a sympathetic ear. Max gave his unfettered opinion, when he cared enough to have one. Talking to Gio was more like trying to cross a field of land mines while blindfolded. It was impossible to guess which word would set Gio off, but an explosion was inevitable.

Gio took his self-appointed role as head of the family seriously—too seriously. It had been the root of many disagreements between them over the years, even if recently they'd called a truce.

A truce that had ended abruptly that morning when Nick had caught his mother crying and had asked her what was wrong. Her answer had infuriated him.

"How is she?" Gio asked smoothly, as if he were inquiring about the weather.

"Weak. The doctor has her on a monitor while they try a new medication."

"I hope he finds what she needs." Gio's comment held just enough sarcasm to renew Nick's earlier anger.

"It would be nice if you pretended to care."

Gio walked over to his desk, sat on the edge of it, and crossed his arms in front of him. "I do, but I'm not convinced she's as ill as she says she is."

"I met with her doctor yesterday. His story matched hers. Is he lying? Am I? What the hell is your problem?"

Gio rubbed his chin with one hand. "She has no history of heart disease and the timing was... convenient."

"Don't you mean inconvenient for you? Afraid if it's true it'll cut down on the time you can spend with your fiancée?"

Gio stood up and dropped his hands to his side. "Leave Julia out of this."

Shaking his head in disgust, Nick said, "I'd like to, but from what I hear she's part of the problem. You may not care what she says to Mother, but I do."

"I have no idea what you're talking about."

"I don't believe you, but that doesn't matter. I came here because you and Julia are upsetting Mother and it's affecting her health. You need to go see her and apologize."

Between gritted teeth, Gio said, "I have nothing to apologize for."

Nick crossed the room and stood nose to nose with his brother. "I could give you a list that goes back years, but right now I'm referring to how you told her she's driving all of us away and will die alone."

Gio's face went white with anger. "I said that because she..." He groaned. "Taken out of context it sounds bad, but..."

"Gio, you said it to an elderly woman who just had a heart attack. There is no context in which that doesn't make you look like a fucking asshole."

Gio rubbed one of his temples. "You don't know the whole story. I didn't tell you what she said to Julia."

"I don't give a shit what she said. I don't care about your little security girlfriend. I care that finally getting laid has you so turned around you can't see how you're hurting our mother."

"The only reason you're still standing is because I know what it's like to be fed lies by her. I feel for you, but if you value your life you won't mention Julia again. Mother doesn't need your protection, trust me."

"So you won't go see her?"

"Not until I'm ready."

Nick shook his head in disgust. "I knew you were a heartless bastard when you threatened to have father's mistress thrown out of her home if she ever contacted us. As long as you get what you want, it doesn't matter who you hurt, does it? Mother wanted to confront her, but you wouldn't let her have that closure, would you? It all has to be on your terms, doesn't it?"

"How long have you known about Leora?"

"I always suspected Father had someone on the side. No one in the oil business needs to spend that much time in Venice. It was why I offered to go with you to collect his body. I wasn't surprised by what you found there. But I was disappointed you didn't think the rest of us deserved the truth."

"You were young..."

"I'm two years younger than you are, Gio. Not a child. You didn't keep us in the dark to protect us—you took advantage of the situation. While Mother grieved, you took over the company. She was so distraught she didn't realize you had no intention of ever giving her back control."

"Is that what she's telling you? You're forgetting I made you a full partner from the beginning. You chose not be involved. You could've joined me at any time. I've kept a goddamned office staffed for you for almost a decade."

"An empty gesture. I tried to work with you when Father first passed. You shut me down every chance you got. Do you know what it was like to speak at a meeting only to have you correct everything I said?"

"You had no idea what you were talking about. I had worked my way up in the company so I knew what needed to be done. You came in with no experience. I couldn't let you—"

"Fuck it up? Or learn enough to be your competition? You don't fool me, Gio. You wanted full control and you got it."

The door of the office opened and Rena strode directly up to the men. "I can hear the two of you in my office. Is everything okay?"

"This is none of your concern, Rena," Gio said without looking away from Nick.

Planting herself directly between them, Rena put her hands on her hips and said, "Yes, it is. I love both of you and that makes it my concern."

Nick put a hand on Rena's shoulder. "We're fine, Rena."

Gio put his hand on Rena's other shoulder and snarled at Nick. "Get your hand off my secretary."

Nick said, "She may work for you, but you don't own her."

"True, but I won't let you use her as another way to piss me off. Rena, stay the hell away from him. Understand me?"

"If Rena and I ever get together it will have nothing to do with you."

"Nick, don't do something I'll have to kill you for."

"Stop it. Both of you." Rena looked back and forth between the two of them and shrugged their hands off. "First of all, I don't belong to anyone, and no one could ever tell me who I could or couldn't see. Second of all, there is no risk of anything happening with Nick because he's practically my brother. Now, what is really going on here?"

Nick met Gio's eyes over Rena's head. "Nothing new."

Gio glared back at him. "I'm not doing this. I'm not getting sucked back into the lies."

"I hoped I could talk you into doing the right thing, Gio, but if you can't be kind to your mother when she's fighting for her life then stay the hell away from her. She doesn't need your version of love."

"I told her what she needed to hear."

"Don't do it again, Gio. Your reign over this family is over. It ends now."

Gio barked a humorless laugh. "Are you threatening me?"

Rena said, "I'm sure that's not what Nick meant."

With a steely voice, Nick said, "Don't test me on this, Gio. You won't win."

Gio ran his hand through his hair. "Nick, you're letting Mother get in your head. This is what she does. She twists things around to suit her agenda. You can't believe anything she says."

"But I can trust you? You're honest with me? Tell me, how long were you going to wait to tell the rest of us we have a half sister?"

His question hung heavy in the room. Gio waved a hand in frustration. "I planned to tell you when we returned from the wedding, but..."

"Really? It's hard to believe anything you say."

"I didn't know about her until I went to see Father's mistress in Venice."

Rena asked, "You have a half sister? Does Luke know?"

Gio's jaw tightened and his face went red with anger. "No. When we returned from Stephan's wedding, we received the call that Mother had had a heart attack and I decided to wait." He clenched and unclenched his hands at his sides. "I didn't want to upset her."

Nick shook his head in disgust. "I can't stomach another moment of this. Stay away from me, Gio. Stay away from all of us or I will take from you the only thing you've ever cared about—Cogent."

❧

"Nick..." Rena said, but Nick was already walking out the office door. As she rushed to follow him, she heard Gio mumbling behind her.

"What the fuck would he do? He doesn't even know where his office is."

Rena sprinted down the hallway after Nick. Years of high school track paid off as she beat him to the elevator door. "Don't go..."

He looked down at her, and the pain in his eyes chased the rest of what she was going to say clear out of her head. Normally he hid behind sarcasm and empty flirtation, but in that moment she saw the man behind the playboy façade, and the sadness in him ripped at her heart. "Stay away from me, Rena. I'm not in a good place."

She took his hand in hers. "That's when you need friends the most. Come back and try talking to Gio again. You're brothers. You can figure this out."

"I wish it were that simple, Rena, but your loyalty to him is misplaced."

"I don't believe that for minute."

"Then you are a poor judge of character." Nick tried to pull his hand away from hers, but Rena held on tighter. She had to make him see that walking away wasn't the answer. When it came to why they didn't get along, neither brother was entirely blameless.

Nick was right: Gio was brutally honest and most comfortable when he was fully in control of a situation. He didn't delegate well and didn't have the patience to wait while others worked out a problem he had already solved. She didn't doubt Nick's version of what it was like to speak at a meeting run by Gio. But she also knew Gio would do anything for his brothers, and that Nick's criticism had hurt him, even if he didn't show it.

Gio was right: Nick hadn't been ready to run the company. Yes, he'd graduated with a business degree from a good university, but he hadn't spent enough time at Cogent to make informed decisions.

Gio should have let Nick make mistakes—and learn from them.

Nick should have worked with Gio instead of turning the situation into a rivalry. Nick could be successful at whatever he chose to do, but maybe he'd have to come out from Gio's shadow to do it. Just as Luke and Max had.

The problem with Gio and Nick was they were more alike than either would acknowledge.

Both too proud.

Too angry.

Too unable to see past the faults in each other.

"I have very good instincts when it comes to people. That's why I know you didn't mean what you said about taking Cogent."

"You think I couldn't do it?"

"No, I know you'd never intentionally hurt your brother. Just like I know you'd never hurt me."

The expression on Nick's face softened. He raised a hand and tucked a lock of hair gently behind Rena's ear. "Take off your rose-colored glasses, Rena. You think everyone has some good in them, but we don't. Not Gio. Not me."

"That's not true, Nick. You came here today because you care about your mother. That's admirable..." *Even if misguided.*

"Stay out of this, Rena. There is no Hallmark card for a family as fucked up as mine is."

Classic Nick. Hurt and lashing out. That got others to back off, but Rena knew him too well. "You can't leave things the way you did. Go back in there and—"

"No. We were both clear enough."

Rena pulled Nick closer, holding both of his arms as she tried to reach past his anger. "No, you weren't. You didn't tell him you love him. You didn't give him time to explain his side of the story. If you did—"

Nick pulled back from Rena abruptly, his eyes burning with anger Rena couldn't understand. "Stay away from me."

There has to be something I can say that will make him see this isn't irreparable. "Luke said he'd come by later today."

"You called him?"

Rena nodded.

"Of course you did. You talk to him more than I do. I'm surprised you've never dated."

"Me and Luke? No. I don't think of him that way."

"Are you sure? The two of you seem to find reasons to slip away to be alone whenever we're all together."

"He's funny. And we're usually talking about—" She stopped before she finished the sentence. She'd almost said, "You." But Nick would take that the wrong way.

She took Nick's hand again and said, "I know you don't like to discuss your family with anyone, but maybe this time you should. I could help you—if you let me."

Nick shook his head. "No."

Rena held on tight, advanced and persisted. "Why not?"

"Because I..." He pulled her into his arms and ravaged her mouth with his. It wasn't how she'd imagined he'd kiss. It was bold and hungry. It may have been meant as a warning or as punishment, but it was too full of passion to be either. He held her face between his hands and plundered. At first she was too surprised to kiss him back, but his touch sparked a heat that rose within her.

This was the kiss she'd always imagined they could share. It had a sizzle, a wildness that swept through both of them, making time and location irrelevant. All that mattered was his mouth, his touch, this fire.

His hands moved down over her, molding her to him with a roughness that only heightened the heat between them. She arched herself against him and felt his erection pulsing against her stomach. His lips left hers and claimed her neck, one hot kiss after another, until all Rena could hear was her own heavy breathing.

And she panicked.

She shoved him back from her and said, "What the hell are you doing, Nick?"

His expression was dark and angry even though his eyes raged with need. He glanced over her shoulder and Rena's confusion grew. She demanded, "Is he there? Don't use me to get back at Gio. I deserve better than that."

He frowned at her accusation but didn't deny it. Without saying a word, he turned and walked away.

One of the secretaries from marketing paused when she saw Rena standing in the hallway and asked, "Rena? Are you okay?"

"I'm fine."

"What are you doing?"

"What?"

"You look like you're waiting for someone."

"No," Rena said with a shake of her head. "Just thinking."

Holy shit, what was that?

Chapter Three

"AND THAT'S WHEN the alien abduction turned ugly and they brought out the probes."

Nick put down his seltzer and pulled his attention away from the crowd below to frown at the red-haired woman next to him in the club's VIP balcony. He'd come there to forget—forget the argument with his brother, and the kiss he'd planted on Rena.

It didn't matter that his brother had deserved everything he'd said to him.

He wasn't proud of how he'd handled the situation.

And Rena.

Fuck, what was I thinking?

He could blame it on the heat of the moment, or on her for cornering him, but he knew the truth: He'd done what he'd wanted to do for a long time and, damn, it had been good. So good he was having a hard time convincing himself repeating it was still a bad idea.

She wanted him as much as he wanted her—that much was obvious from the kiss. So, what was stopping them? Gio? Kane?

Fuck them.

"What did you say?" he asked the irritated beauty, who was waiting for him to answer her.

She flipped her hair over one shoulder and huffed. The action revealed a long bare expanse of neck that yesterday would have been a temptation. She was dressed in a pricier version of the skintight, attention-getting bits of material worn by the masses below. If he cared enough to ask her, he'd bet she could tell him who made it. But he didn't—care, that is. He couldn't remember how he'd met her, but they'd hung out in the past. Even fucked a few times. But she meant nothing to him.

He hadn't asked her to join him that night. She'd followed him when she saw him walking up the stairs. How much she was or wasn't entertained wasn't of much importance to him.

And she knew it. "Have you been listening to me at all?"

Nick had done many things in his life he wasn't proud of, but he wasn't a liar, and he had no patience for those who were. "No."

"What's your problem tonight?"

Nick shrugged and turned to look down at the crowd below. He had a growing list of issues but none he wanted to discuss with her. He wasn't about to tell her anything personal, so any reference to his brother or mother was not possible. He doubted she wanted to hear about Rena.

I wanted to be alone tonight. To some, finding solace at Club Skal might have sounded like a contradiction, but he was more comfortable there than anywhere else. Serge Boyd, the club's owner, had even given him his own VIP section for his twenty-first birthday.

Not long ago Nick would have turned the balcony into a party that would have gone on until dawn. None of his friends wanted to grow up to be king or CEO. They were famous for being young, rich, and wild. Who wants to be first in line, when second has all the fun with none of the responsibility? For a long time he'd lived by that philosophy, but something had clicked within him when he'd been with his brothers on Isola Santos, the island of his ancestors. He'd stood there with generations of his family, many of whom had built successful financial empires or birthed football teams' worth of new Andrades, and felt ashamed of the path he'd chosen. At the wedding reception, his uncles had spoken of family members who had passed—his own father in particular. They'd told stories of how each generation of Andrade worked hard to make sure the next was taken care of, and how proud Gio Sr. must be when he looked down on his sons.

Proud of me? I don't think so.

I've done nothing with my life.

That realization had given way to another one: *And I won't if I keep drinking.*

He hadn't touched a drop of alcohol since.

The woman moved to stand in front of him and said, "I know how to cheer you up." She leaned down, placing her hands on both of his shoulders, and hovered her lips just above his. "Remember that night at Siviti's?"

He did, but the memory didn't move him or his cock. He took her hands in his and stood. "It's been a long day, Melissa. You should—"

Her face went red and she pulled her hands from his. "My name isn't Melissa."

Fuck.

"Like I said—long day. I came here to clear my head."

She stood before him angrily and stared up at him, refusing to let him off the hook until he remembered her name. He tried, but the times they had spent together had always been after he'd given himself over to a substantial buzz.

If she'd ever said her name, he hadn't heard it.

And it had never mattered until just then. *I think it starts with an M...*

"Michelle..."

"Megan," the woman hissed. "My name is *Megan*." She reached down, picked up her drink, and threw it at the front of his pants.

Nick jumped back, but it was too late. The vodka darkened a large circle around his crotch and spread down one leg. He grabbed a napkin from the table and wiped as much off as he could. "Why the fuck would you do that?"

Megan stood angrily in front of him. "Maybe now you'll remember me."

Shaking his head, Nick said coldly, "Get out."

With a snarl, Megan said, "You used to be fun. No wonder you're alone tonight. You've been a real drag lately."

Nick merely raised one eyebrow, then looked at the stairs leading back down to the club. His meaning was clear.

Megan's beauty diminished as her features twisted. "What a waste of time. I should have slept with Harry instead of you. At least I could have said I fucked a prince."

After she left, Nick looked down at his pants and swore. The damp area was much darker than the rest of his pants. If she'd poured it on any other part of his body he would have walked out of the club and gone back to his hotel room to change, but photo hounds would love a picture of him looking like he pissed himself. He took out his cell phone, called downstairs, and spoke to the club owner. "Do you have a spare pair of pants down there?"

"Should I ask why?" Serge joked.

Nick wasn't in the mood to tell Serge, but not because he thought it would surprise him. Nothing shocked Serge. He often said Nick reminded him of himself when he was younger, back before he'd created Skal. There were worse people Nick could imagine himself becoming. Serge was well known for owning a successful club that was packed every night with regulars drawn from the global Who's Who list.

And when Nick was in town, he was one of them.

"A spilled drink. Nothing big, but I do need a change of pants or the use of your dryer downstairs."

"I'll send someone up for your clothes. I can't have you in the kitchen half dressed or my staff will get nothing done."

"Thanks." There was a time when Nick's popularity with women had been a badge of pride for him. None of that mattered anymore.

Before hanging up, Serge asked, "Nick, are you okay?"

"Yeah. Just wet."

"I'm talking about you, not your pants. You haven't been the same since you came back from that wedding. All you do is sit up there and sulk. Why not invite some of your friends by? Being alone isn't good for you."

"I told you I gave up drinking."

"And how is that working out for you?"

"People are a lot more annoying when I'm sober."

Serge chuckled. "That's why I imbibe."

"Apparently I'm not as much fun as I used to be. I'm surprised you haven't rescinded my VIP status."

"Never. You're like a son to me, Nick. You and I, we belong here."

A heavy feeling settled over Nick. "Do we? I don't know anymore."

"You know what your problem is?"

"Please, enlighten me."

"You need to stay the hell away from your family. Stop trying to figure them out. You'll only make yourself crazy. Do you want me to send up some girls? There are plenty downstairs who would jump at the invite."

"Not tonight."

"If you change your mind, call me. I don't like to see you like this."

"I'll be in a much better mood when I have dry pants."

"Okay, okay. I'll send someone up for your clothes."

Nick hung up, kicked off his shoes, and undid the top of his pants. The front of his shirt was damp, too, so he removed that as well. Thankfully, his boxer briefs were dry. He handed his clothing to the blushing cocktail waitress who appeared minutes later, then returned to his table with his seltzer water. He reached for it with a sigh.

Megan wasn't the first to express discontent with him since he'd stopped drinking. His large circle of friends was shrinking fast. People he'd hung out with for more than a decade were more interested in getting on the list to the next big party than remaining in touch with him if he wasn't going to be throwing it.

They said they were worried about him.

One phone call to anyone in that social circle could have had the balcony full of beautiful women and men who claimed to care about him. Maybe a few drinks didn't matter one way or another. They'd take the edge off his anger—just as they had a hundred times before.

No, the cost of a night of excess would be facing himself in the mirror the next day and asking himself—once again—what he had ever done that his father would be proud of.

Why the hell do I care what a man like my father would think about anything? He was a liar and a cheat, and the biggest favor he did any of us was to die and reveal his double life.

Nick closed his eyes and thought back to his confrontation with Gio. It had gone badly, but that was nothing new for them. He didn't care what Gio thought of him as long as he'd gotten his message. Their mother had been through enough. She'd survived the loss of her parents, the rejection of her in-laws, the death of her husband, and the realization that his infidelity had been substantial. Now she was facing her own mortality—and Gio was attacking her. It didn't make sense, but it did need to end.

When Nick had given up drinking, he'd mistakenly imagined it would bring him closer to his family. Instead, he was consumed with a level of anger he hadn't felt since his father had died.

He hated that he kept going over what Gio had said. Why wouldn't their mother let Luke look at her medical records? He didn't want her to be ill, but he didn't want to discover she'd fabricated her heart attack, either.

Serge was right. His family made him nuts.

He'd already failed as the good brother he'd temporarily convinced himself he could be. He was quickly proving himself to be a complete washout as a devoted son. *I'm alone in my underwear in a dance club. Is this what they call rock bottom?*

The temptation to call downstairs for a bottle of anything was strong, but Nick fought it and sipped his seltzer instead. He didn't need a drink.

He needed something more distracting than a hangover.

Or someone.

He remembered the desire in Rena's eyes even as she'd chastised him for kissing her. He could still taste her on his lips—still feel how she had arched against him, eager for more.

He left behind the unpleasantness of his day and gave himself to the fantasy of what he would do if she came to finish what their kiss had started. He'd push the prim hemline of her skirt up and slide his fingers into her while he fucked her mouth with his tongue. He wanted to watch her come again and again before finally sinking into her and taking his own pleasure.

C3

Rena bypassed the line outside Skal and spoke directly to the bouncer. She asked if he'd seen Nick Andrade. He looked her over, then wordlessly dismissed her.

A quick glance down reminded her that she was still dressed in the gray skirt and white blouse she'd worn to work. *Could I look less like I belong here?* She flashed him a smile she reserved for just such situations. Her family was immune to it, but it had gotten her out of a fair share of traffic tickets. One of her old boyfriends had called it her "get out of jail smile." She was sure it didn't wield that level of power, but if she ever found herself sitting in a cell, she'd certainly test it.

At first she thought she'd lost her touch. The man frowned down at her. She beamed her smile at him again. Suddenly, with a curt nod, he stepped aside for her to enter. She stepped inside, and immediately her senses were assailed by loud music. Skal had a reputation for bringing Vegas-like wildness to the elite crowd of New York. No one entered unless they knew someone. The dance floor was packed, as were the darkened areas around it. Above the dance floor, two semi-private balconies looked down over the crowd. One was full of people. The other appeared empty.

Nick was in one of those VIP sections. Of that, Rena was certain.

She had decided to try the busy one until she glimpsed movement in the other. Someone was having a private party. Rena paused and touched a hand to her lips.

Was Nick up there with a woman?

Does it matter? No.

He kissed me, but that was to shut me up... or prove something to his brother. Gio should have never told him to stay away from me. Telling Nick not to do something was like waving candy before a toddler and then trying to convince him to wait until after dinner to eat it.

The kiss meant nothing.

I'm over it.

The outside wall of the club led to a stairway that looked as if it led up to the balconies, but it was roped off. Rena put her hand on the clasp of the rope and hesitated, mentally rehearsing what she would say to Nick.

Fresh from a conversation with Luke, where he'd reiterated his warning about putting herself between his brothers, Rena was even more determined she had to. Gio had looked defeated when Nick had stormed out of his office. His mood hadn't improved even after Luke had spoken to him. It had taken a call from his fiancée, Julia, to get Gio to go home.

He was worried about his brothers, and he had reason to be. Whatever understanding they had come to in Italy had crumbled since they'd come home. She wanted to see them the way they'd been directly after their return. They'd laughed. Teased each other. For Rena, it had felt as if she'd gone back in time to when she'd first met them—back before their father had died.

To see them revert to mistrust was heartbreaking. It was the same old story, except this time, Patrice had declared Gio the villain and Nick her champion. For Nick, someone who had been considered the black sheep of his family for so long, it would have felt good to finally be in a position of favor. Patrice knew exactly how to play her sons against each other. Rena shuddered just thinking about her. Something cold had taken root in that woman's heart and it had consumed her. Love should be unconditional, but in the Andrade household Rena had visited, it was given and withheld deliberately.

Everyone had some good in them, but in Patrice it was buried deep—really deep—if it was still there at all.

"Are you looking for someone?" a male voice asked from behind her.

With her hand still on the rope, Rena turned and forced a smile to her lips. The man who'd addressed her was an older gentleman who looked to be in his late fifties. He wore an open-collared white shirt and dark pants and spoke with a slight accent and an easy confidence.

Lying boldly, Rena said, "Nick Andrade asked me to drop by. Is he upstairs?"

The man raised one eyebrow and Rena blinked quickly, her sudden confidence diffusing. "He did?"

"Yes, he..." Rena stopped herself there. He wasn't buying her story. Would the truth sway him? "Okay, he didn't invite me, but I need to talk to him." When the man continued to silently watch her, she softened her tone. "Please."

"Interesting." He gave her another once-over as if evaluating a puzzle piece. "I've never seen you here before. How well do you know him?"

Rena met his eyes with the bold honesty that was her nature. "Very well."

"What is he allergic to?"

His question took Rena by surprise, but she answered without missing a beat. "Shellfish. It gives him a rash."

The man nodded in approval. "It does. You explain a lot."

"I'm sorry?"

"Where are my manners?" The man held out his hand. "My name is Sergey Boyd, but you can me Serge. Tell me, how long have you been seeing Nick?"

Rena blushed beneath his scrutiny. "We aren't... we're not... we're just friends."

"Friends." He made a sound of disbelief deep in his throat. "I don't believe men and women can just be friends. One always wants something more."

Rena raised her chin and met his eyes. "I'm sorry your experiences have jaded you, but I don't agree."

"So there has never been anything between you and Nick?" He watched her reaction closely and Rena cursed herself for blushing.

"Not that it is any of your business, but no. Never."

"What's your name?"

"Rena Sander."

An enigmatic smile spread across his face. "I've heard of you."

Don't ask. Don't do it. Oh, what the hell. "You have?"

He stepped forward and unclasped the rope, holding it to one side to let her pass. "This leads to a landing. Go left at the top. You'll find Nick there." His eyes lit with a private joke.

Rena paused. "Is there something I should know?"

He shrugged and refastened the rope behind her. "Rena, next time you come here, you tell whoever is at the door that you are four-one-one."

"What am I?" She wasn't sure she wanted to know the answer to that question either. When Serge answered with a wink, Rena squared her shoulders and said, "I won't be back anyway."

He didn't argue the point, but he was still smiling when she turned and headed up the stairs.

The music from below boomed through the hallway, and Rena could feel the bass echoing through her as she walked. She wondered what her brother, Kane, would say if he knew where she was. Most likely, he'd magically appear before she had time to reach the top step. By some people's definition, her family was overprotective.

Her father had always said, "Money comes and goes, youth and health will one day leave you, but family endures. In the end, it's all that really matters."

They loved her and, therefore, they did everything they could to keep her safe. How could she resent them for that?

She'd seen firsthand the dangerous temptations that came with being wealthy. More than a few of her old friends from high school cited boredom as the reason they indulged in self-destructive behaviors. Well into their twenties, they still wrecked cars, slept with each other's boyfriends, and partied in VIP areas where they could do as they pleased without the prying eyes of the public.

Nick was part of that world.

The door to the balcony on the left was open. Rena took a step inside the room and looked around. Nick was standing beside a table with his back to her, just back far enough from the wooden railing that he wouldn't be visible to those below.

Her breath caught in her throat as she soaked in the perfection of the mostly nude man before her. His dark boxer briefs clung to his tight ass and hugged his muscular thighs. She wouldn't have been human if she hadn't taken a moment to appreciate the cut of his bare back and the breadth of the strong shoulders above it. Apparently he worked out as hard as he partied.

Oh, God.

I told Serge he was wrong; I lied. I'm a bad, bad friend. I do want more.

I always have, no matter what I've told myself.

The intensity of her attraction to him made Rena nervous, and she began to babble internally.

Hello, I'm lost. Can anyone tell me how to get back to denial?

It's a beautiful place located in the land of sanity. You know, where things make sense and I don't leer at men in their underwear?

Nick picked up a glass of clear liquid and the napkin beneath it fluttered to the floor. He bent to retrieve it. Rena bit her lower lip as he did. The movement rippled the muscles in his back and thighs. Mouth dry, Rena imagined running her hands over both.

She let out a wistful sigh that echoed through the room.

Nick froze, straightened, and turned. Their eyes met across the room. Unable to deny herself, Rena let her gaze slide down his lightly haired chest, over his well-defined abs, to a part of him the dark briefs outlined lovingly.

Damn, no wonder women lined up to date him. Even in an unaroused state, his size was enough to make her jaw go slack. She knew she should look away, but he stirred beneath her scrutiny and an answering heat swept through her.

Whoa.

Just, whoa.

In slow motion, Rena raised her eyes. She expected him to be amused, but the expression on his face was anything but jovial. He'd never looked at her that way before. One kiss had changed everything.

And nothing, she reminded herself harshly.

It's not surprising he wants me. She shook her head and squared her shoulders. *I'm a woman and I'm breathing—that's his criteria. Add to that how he was told I'm off-limits and I'm suddenly on his who-to-do list. Do not read anything into it. This is Nick we're talking about. He'd do a nun just to say he had. And he either just screwed someone or was just about to. Either way, I need to stop looking at his amazing abs and start reminding myself why being with him, even one time, would be a mistake.*

And I will, right after I give myself a moment to enjoy how it feels to be wanted by a man like him. Yeowza.

Rena swallowed hard as Nick closed the distance between them. He stopped less than a foot from her. Close enough that, had she raised her hand, she could have touched the smooth muscles of his chest. Close enough that she could feel the heat emanating from his body.

"What are you doing here, Rena?" The warm timbre of his voice made her skin tingle with anticipation. A woman couldn't be blamed for the naughty thoughts that raced through her head when he used that tone.

I'm here because he needs tough love. Focus. Rena gathered her inner resolve, calmed her libido, and asked, "Can we talk?" She quickly scanned the room. "What I have to say won't take long. Then you can go back to your *party*."

"No party," he said, his expression becoming guarded. "I'm alone."

The way he said *alone* sent her thoughts scattering, and she frowned. Her feelings for him were a complicated mix of yearning and caring. She wanted to hug him and tell him that everything was going to be okay. She wanted to throw herself into his arms and lose herself in his kiss again. Her body had never hummed for a man the way it did right then for Nick. She licked her bottom lip.

He's a piece of chocolate cake in my fridge at midnight. Regret will trump any pleasure found in giving in to the temptation of him. Not to mention, he's half naked for someone else. "I'm surprised your date left so early."

"I didn't have a date."

"Really?" She looked down at his boxers again, which were now straining to contain his growing excitement. She'd thought he was big before, but the current size of him took her breath away, and she blushed as images of what he'd look like without that thin layer of cotton filled her head. She looked off to one side. "Go put your pants on."

A sexy chuckle rumbled in his chest. "Are you finding it difficult to concentrate?"

Rena took a step back and put her hands on her hips. "This isn't funny, Nick."

A roguish smile spread across his face, revealing dimples rarely displayed. He took a step closer. "I'm not laughing. Why are you here, Rena?"

Rena held her ground and straightened her shoulders defiantly. "I told you. We have to talk."

"About the kiss?" He raised a hand and traced the line of her jaw lightly with the back of one finger. "The only reason you'd come all this way to discuss it is if you wanted another." His finger moved upward to gently trace the outline of her lips.

She opened her mouth to deny it, but his finger slid inside and traced the wet softness just inside her bottom lip. She flicked the tip of her tongue across his finger. His eyes darkened and his breathing deepened.

I did not mean to do that.

He held her eyes and moved his finger deeper into her mouth. He circled the tip of her tongue playfully, caressing it, exploring it. "Do you even know what you want, Rena? Do you want me to show you?" She closed her lips around his finger.

He withdrew his hand and pulled her fully against him. He held her there, pressed against his need for her, and growled sexily into her ear, "I was thinking a little lower."

Rena raised her hands to push him away, but when her hands met his bare shoulders her fingers dug into them. He felt so good beneath her hands. She wanted to touch more, but instead she kept her hands still while she fought for sanity. "This isn't why I came here."

"We're not children anymore." He took one of her hands from his shoulder and slid it beneath the band of his boxers. "You can take what you want."

He was hard and ready and the width of him sent her heart beating wildly in her chest. Her hand automatically ran up and down his pulsing cock, exploring the length of him. She'd never been with a man of his size, and in a frenzy of desire she wondered if it would be as good as magazines claimed it was.

Take what you want.

Sex was something that happened between two people who had reached a certain level of commitment. It was gentle and sweet. And that's how Rena liked it. Or at least that was what she had always told herself.

This was different.

This was lust. Pure and simple.

It overshadowed everything else.

She tried to withdraw her hand, but he laid his hand over hers, holding her there against him. Rubbing her hand up and down along his pulsing shaft. "Are you afraid, Rena? You don't have to be. I would fuck you until you couldn't remember the name of anyone before me. I'd make you come so many times you'd think of me every time you pleasure yourself."

She wanted to be offended by how he was talking to her, but she couldn't deny how it aroused her. "I don't do that," she whispered. Her admission was rewarded by an excited clench of his hand over hers.

"You will," he promised, and his mouth swept down and claimed hers. His tongue boldly pushed between her lips and claimed hers. He sucked gently, rhythmically, until hers engaged with his fully in an intimate dance. Meanwhile, his hand moved hers up and down against him until she was caressing him urgently on her own.

Rena gasped when he expertly unbuttoned her blouse and kissed his way down her neck to her nipples, which were pointing eagerly through the thin silk of her bra. He nipped at them, tugging on them, even through the material. Rena threw her head back and with one hand held his head to her.

There was a crash of a chair behind them and Rena jumped out of Nick's arms. She turned in time to see a blushing cocktail waitress righting a chair and picking clothing off the floor. "I'm so sorry," the woman said. "I didn't see you at first. I was going to leave the clothes on the table for you, Mr. Andrade, but I can bring them back later."

"Leave them," Nick growled.

The intrusion was a splash of reality for Rena. She hastily rebuttoned her shirt and tucked it back into her skirt. She wasn't the type who embarrassed easily, but then she'd never done anything like this before.

What the hell am I doing?
What was I thinking?
I wasn't.
That's the problem.

I let one kiss completely unravel me.

I'm at a club, for God's sake. I don't do things like this.

She stole a glance at Nick after the waitress left but couldn't decipher his expression. Was he angry? Frustrated? "Sorry about that," he said.

"Sorry about what? That you mauled me?" She was unable to keep anger out of her voice. When he approached her, she retreated and said wildly, "Don't touch me."

He advanced and she backed away until she was against the side of a table. He took her chin in one hand and forced her eyes to his. "You came to me, Rena. Don't pretend you didn't enjoy that kiss or you weren't open to where it was going. I'd be inside you right now if we hadn't been interrupted, and you'd be digging your nails into my back and calling out my name."

She couldn't help but imagine them intimately entwined the way he described. *Would I have gone that far? Shamelessly? Right here?* She licked her bottom lip nervously. "That's not true."

He bent closer, and her eyelids lowered in anticipation of his mouth claiming hers again. The first touch was the briefest of touches, just enough to make her quiver with need. "Oh, my little Rena, you know it is. And there is no reason we can't continue what we started. I've wanted you for a long time, and tonight I could use the distraction."

Distraction? That's all it would be to him?

A myriad of unpleasant emotions swelled up and stamped back the desire raging within her. *I am such an idiot.* Rena raised her hand and slapped him across the face. His head reeled back and his nostrils flared angrily.

She'd never hit anyone in her whole life. "You deserved that," she said, trying not to sound sorry even though she'd instantly regretted her action.

He rubbed a hand thoughtfully over his reddened cheek. "Maybe."

Rena hugged her arms protectively around her waist. "I'm sorry I hit you."

A rueful smile curled one side of his lips. "Don't be, because then I'll have to say I'm sorry I kissed you, and I'm not. I'm not sorry at all."

"Stop. I don't want to play this game. I don't know if you're coming on to me because you think being with me would upset Gio, or if I'm some stand-in for whoever walked out on you. I don't know, and I don't care. This..." Rena waved one hand between them wildly, "cannot happen."

Nick's jaw tightened and his eyes narrowed. "I would never use you to get back at Gio."

Rena closed her eyes and sighed, then opened them and said, "I want to believe that."

"You can." He rubbed a hand harshly over his forehead with frustration when Rena stared at him silently. "What are you waiting for me to say?"

Giving herself an internal smack, Rena shook her head. *What am I waiting for? Some explanation of why he is in his boxers that has nothing to do with being with another woman? I am royally screwed up.* "Nothing. Not a damn thing. But I do expect you to listen to me for a minute. You need to call Gio tonight. You need to apologize to him and work this out. You're almost thirty, Nick. Look at you. Is this really all you want from your life?"

"What gives you the goddamn right to come here and judge me? Just who the fuck do you think you are?"

His words stung, but Rena didn't let them stop her from saying what she'd come to say. She held out a hand. "Who am I? Nick, we've been friends for most of our lives. I love you"— Nick's eyebrows shot up, then his head snapped back as she continued—"and your brothers. I hate to see any of you unhappy."

Nick let out a long audible breath. "Go home, Rena."

Rena hesitated. She didn't want to leave, but she knew she couldn't stay. "Nick..."

"Do us both a favor and don't come back."

There was a finality to his tone that shook Rena. A tear rolled down her cheeks as she inwardly cursed herself for believing she could convince him to do anything—and for how close she'd come to making a monumental mistake.

Luke had warned her she'd get hurt, but she'd believed that beneath all of his bad-boy bravado there was a good man looking for a way to break free. Maybe there wasn't.

And I'm a fool who sees only what I want to see.

"Rena—" Nick called out, but she continued down the stairs.

ঙ

Nick wasn't a man who chased a woman, yet he found himself racing after her. There wasn't a part of what had just happened that he didn't regret. He'd been in a foul mood, plus Rena had walked in just when he'd revved himself up fantasizing about what they'd almost just done upstairs.

Shit. Shit. Shit.

He'd never meant to hurt her. He caught up with her in front of the bar near the dance floor. She was walking away with long purposeful strides. He grabbed one of her arms to stop her, and her momentum swung her around and crashed her into his chest. He steadied her with a hand on either arm. "I'm an ass," he stated flatly, leaning in close to her ear to be heard above the music.

She pushed against his chest, but he didn't release her. "Yes, you are."

"I shouldn't have taken my bad mood out on you."

Her lips pressed angrily together for a moment longer, then softened. "No, you shouldn't have, but I shouldn't have tried to talk to you about this while you were out drinking. I could have waited until tomorrow."

"I don't," he said, loving how she leaned in to hear his words. "I've been sober for three months. I didn't come here to party. I needed somewhere I could think."

She cocked a skeptical eyebrow at him. "In your underwear?"

He looked down. "Shit." A quick look around confirmed his lack of clothing had not gone unnoticed. People all around them were taking photos with their phones. He put a hand up to shield her face from them, even though he knew it was already too late. When he looked down at her again he shook his head and gave a self-disgusted grunt. He didn't know if he should drag her back upstairs or bolt with her to the door. Either way, there was no changing one fact. "This is going to be in the papers tomorrow."

Instead of looking mortified, as he'd thought she would, she cocked her head to one side and her forehead creased thoughtfully. "Did you really give up drinking?"

He nodded. "It was time."

Her eyes were bright with emotion when she said, "I'm proud of you." Then she pulled his face down to hers and kissed him boldly.

He was staring down at her in bemusement when she ended the kiss.

She winked at him. "I refuse to be the only woman you've been photographed with *not* kissing."

Then she turned and walked away, leaving him stunned and speechless before a crowd of snap-happy amateur photographers. He shook his head, smiled, and started back toward his VIP section. He didn't care if they continued to photograph him.

Hell, he'd been caught in much more compromising situations. All he cared about was how he'd felt when Rena had smiled up at him with pride. In her eyes he saw the man he'd always thought he could be, always feared he wasn't. When she'd looked at him that way, for just that one moment, everything and anything seemed possible.

Rena was long gone by the time Nick returned to the bar fully clothed. He was headed toward a side exit when Serge stepped into his path.

"Your friend left?"

"I'll see her again."

Serge raised one hand in caution. "Don't, Nick."

Nick threw up two hands. "Why do you care?"

"She has feelings for you. Don't take advantage of that."

"I have no intention to. Hell, I've known Rena most of my life. I would never hurt her."

"Then stay as far away from her as you can. Call that saucy redhead. Anyone. You won't mean to hurt her, but you will—and then you'll have to live with what you've done."

"You think I'm too fucked up for her?"

"I didn't say that, Nick. You did. I'm simply suggesting if you care about this one, stay the hell away from her." Serge walked away, and Nick punched the wall beside the door as he walked out of the club.

Chapter Four

RENA WOKE TO her doorbell ringing over and over again. She rolled over and groaned. *Am I late to work? No, it's Saturday. Who would bang on my door this early on a weekend?*

She sat straight up in bed and pulled the hem of her nightshirt down over her thighs. *Nick.* She reached for her phone and saw she had four missed calls. *Not Nick. Madison D'Argenson, Nick's cousin.* She'd sent a couple of texts after Rena hadn't answered her calls. *Shit, I made plans with her for this morning.*

She scrambled out of bed, tried to tame her hair in the mirror, then gave up and headed downstairs. "Coming. One minute."

She looked down at her nightshirt, shook her head, and opened the door while forcing a smile. "Maddy, I slept in by accident. I'm so sorry."

Maddy didn't seem the least bit bothered by Rena's disheveled state. She held up a tray of coffees and a bag of baked goods. "Bagel? Muffin? I wasn't sure so I brought both." She was surprisingly energetic for a woman who had had her second child less than a month before. "I have one hour while Adam naps and Richard gives Joey a cooking lesson."

"Isn't he young for that?"

"It's important for Richard to spend time with him, and my husband loves to talk about cooking. They make pastries and crepes together. It's adorable, and it gives me an hour of sanity away from them."

Behind her, Nicole Andrade, the newest addition to the clan and Stephan's wife, shyly ducked her head in. She was, as always, impeccably attired in an exclusive designer dress. She was also, of the two women visiting Rena, the only one who looked sincerely apologetic. She laid a hand on Maddy's arm. "Maddy, Rena doesn't look like she's ready for company. Maybe we should come back."

It always amazed Rena that someone as beautiful and wealthy as Nicole could be unsure of herself. Her heart went out to Nicole, and any self-consciousness Rena had felt about welcoming visitors in her nightshirt fell aside. She opened the door wider, saying, "If you don't mind, I don't mind. Come in."

"See," Maddy said over her shoulder with a wide smile. "Rena and I became close when I started my campaign to bring Gio to your wedding. Now we're like this." She held up two crossed fingers.

The complete opposite of Nicole, Maddy happily plowed through life—as comfortable in her own skin as she was with refusing to hear the word *no*. She had an optimism that, while grating at first, was enviable. She was also a bit of a meddler, which Rena admired about her. She was the reason the Andrade brothers had attended Stephan's wedding in Italy.

Rena held up her own crossed fingers and referenced the way she was dressed as she led the two women to her living room. "Luckily we're this close. Not everyone gets to see me without makeup."

Nicole blushed. "When you didn't answer your phone I thought you might still be sleeping. I told Maddy we should wait, but you know how she is."

Maddy placed the tray and bag on the living room coffee table, then plopped down into one of the chairs. "You'll understand when you have children. This morning was a scheduled break. I'm am not losing my hour of adult time for anyone."

Rena settled into a chair across from her. "I'm surprised you don't have a nanny."

Maddy took out a muffin and laid it on a napkin, then handed a coffee container to Rena. "Black with sugar. That's how you like it, isn't it?"

"Yes," Rena said with surprise. She and Maddy had spent a significant amount of time on the phone over the last several months, yet their friendship was still in the early stages. "Thank you for remembering."

Nicole hovered, then sat and took her own coffee. "She does have a nanny, but she refuses to let her do much."

Maddy shrugged. "I whine now and then, but there isn't a single part of my life that I would change. Richard is doing well with his restaurants. I love being home with the boys. Okay, most of the time. I don't think there is a mother alive who doesn't sometimes crave a few moments to herself. I could hand them off to the nanny more, but when they look back at their childhood I want them to remember me more than someone we paid to be with them. That's how my parents raised me, and that's how I'm raising my children. I won't apologize for that."

Rena sipped her coffee, then said, "You shouldn't. Your children are lucky to have you." She turned to Nicole, who was eating her bagel as daintily as if she were visiting the Queen. "How is married life, Nicole? Enjoying it?"

Nicole put her bagel down and folded her hands in her lap. Her eyes misted over as she said, "It's still unbelievable to me—how much my life has changed in just a couple of years." She reached out and took Maddy's hand in hers. "Even Maddy. She is crazy, but I can't imagine not having her in my life."

Maddy squeezed her hand and shot her a huge smile. "We feel the same way about you, Nicole. Well, we don't call you crazy, but you fit into our family perfectly. And Stephan is finally happy. Love can do that."

Rena took another sip of her coffee.

"Which brings us to why we're here, Rena," Maddy continued. "Can you help us find the perfect woman for Nick?"

Rena gasped, choked on her coffee, and started coughing wildly. Nicole leaned over and gave her a pat on the back. "I'm sorry," she said when she caught her breath. "I swallowed the wrong way."

"I hate when that happens," Maddy said sympathetically, oblivious to Rena's state of surprise.

After a brief pause, Rena asked, "What makes you think Nick needs help finding a woman? He certainly seems to surround himself with enough of them."

"He's not happy." Maddy shook her head sadly. "And look at how hard he's taking his mother's illness. You'd expect he'd be concerned, but he's just miserable with worry. He needs someone in his life he can lean on when times are tough. Everyone does." She rolled her eyes. "And I'm not talking about the bimbos he's always photographed with. I'm talking about someone of quality. You know him well. What does he look for in a woman?"

"A low IQ and huge cleavage." Even as the words came out of Rena's mouth she regretted them. *After what happened last night, I'm in no position to judge anyone.* "I'm sorry. That was rude of me. Trust me, though. Nick isn't looking for anything serious with anyone."

"That's a shame," Maddy said and took a bite of her muffin.

"Why?"

Maddy leaned forward and tapped Nicole's leg. "We should tell her."

"How are we going to win if we keep telling everyone everything?" Nicole asked with a laugh.

"Tell me what?"

Nicole shrugged and nodded at Maddy.

Maddy wiped her hands on a napkin. "I'll tell you, but you have to keep this to yourself. Do I have your word?"

Rena looked back and forth between them. "I think so."

Nicole wrung her hands in front of her. "You have to promise to keep our secret. Stephan wouldn't like the idea of us meddling like we are."

Maddy gave an exasperated sigh. "You worry too much about what Stephan thinks. If he gets upset, he'll get over it. Who could stay mad at us?"

With a sad smile, Nicole added, "I wish I could see the world like you do, Maddy, but we had very different childhoods. I've never been part of a family like yours. They are so loving and supportive. I don't ever want to do anything that would take them away from me."

Rena blinked back tears and pretended to reach for a bagel.

Maddy scooted closer and hugged Nicole. "No one is going anywhere. You're stuck with us."

Nicole hugged her back and composed herself. "We didn't wake Rena up for this. Let's just lay it out there and then let her get on with her day."

Maddy said, "Rena, you don't have to swear on a Bible or anything, just keep this between us, okay?"

Curiosity piqued, Rena gave one curt.

"Nicole and I are on the same team..."

"Team?"

Nicole interjected, "It all started as a joke at Lil and Jake's wedding. Then it grew."

"What grew?" Rena asked.

"I was telling everyone how much I missed Gio, Nick, Luke, and Max, and we sort of all decided that helping them find love would bring them back to the family."

"You decided," Nicole gently reminded.

Maddy smiled and shrugged. "Anyway, all the women are in on it. Dominic's wife, Abby, has teamed up with Marie. Her sister, Lil, is working with her best friend, Alethea. Nicole and I are pooling our resources. Whoever matches one of the cousins up with someone he decides to marry, wins."

"Wins what?"

As if it should have been obvious, Maddy rolled her eyes. "The right to call themselves the best matchmaker in the family. Until now it's always been me, and I am not giving up my title easily."

As Rena processed this, she said slowly, "So Julia, Gio's fiancée, was your doing?"

Nicole shook her head. "No, none of us knew her."

Maddy clapped her hands together. "Isn't that what makes this amazing? She was an unknown and took the prize.... It was as if the universe planted its own contender."

"Planted?" Rena closed her eyes and covered her mouth with one hand as a realization came to her. "Those beautiful women who started getting hired at Cogent... you did that?"

Nicole folded her napkin carefully in her lap. "We helped it happen, but not all of them are ours. Lil and Alethea sent the IT woman."

Maddy slapped a hand on the cushion beside her. "So, no one won round one. Except Gio, because he looks happy with Julia. But we have three chances left. And I think Nick is our best bet. Especially if you join our team. No one knows the brothers better than you do. You could help us hone our choices. Please. Say you'll do it."

Is this punishment for the kiss I gave Nick in front of all the photographers? Someone sure has a sick sense of humor. Rena didn't believe for a moment that Maddy or Nicole knew anything about what had gone on between Nick and her.

And there is no way I'm telling them. "I don't think—"

Maddy leaned forward to drive her argument home. "Love makes everything better. I'm not suggesting that we force anyone on him. We're merely surrounding him with possibilities. That's all love needs—a chance to happen. Look at how much happier Gio is now that he found his match. Don't you want the same for Nick?"

Rena stood up. "It's an awful idea and I won't help you." *I can't help Nick fall in love with someone else.*

Maddy gathered up the leftover food and placed it in the bag. She looked offended, and Rena didn't see a way she could explain herself without revealing how confused she was about last night. She was worried enough about how she was going to weather the storm that would arise if the pictures surfaced somewhere. "Maddy, I'm sorry."

Maddy gathered her purse. "Don't be. I shouldn't have expected you to understand."

Nicole took Rena by the hand, leaned in, and whispered, "She doesn't like the word *no*. Don't worry. I'll talk to her."

Giving herself a mental shake, Maddy smiled. "Rena, your problem is that you haven't been around me enough to trust my genius. I'm right about this. When Nick finds someone who loves him for who he is, his whole world will change. You watch. We'll find the perfect woman for him. They'll be so damn happy together we'll see them all the time, just like Julia and Gio. I'm never wrong about this stuff. I can understand why you are hesitant now. But you'll see. And then you can team up with us to find someone for Luke."

After Maddy and Nicole left, Rena leaned against the door and let out a long sigh. Her cell phone vibrated with a cryptic text.

On my way over. We need to talk. Kane.

Rena took the stairs to her bedroom two at a time. *Looks like today is going from bad to worse. If I'm to have any chance of surviving it, I'd better shower.*

Thirty minutes later, Rena greeted her brother at the door. *Round two.* At least she'd had time to wake up and get dressed. Amazing what a good pants suit and the right makeup can do for a person's confidence. "Kane, I thought you were driving up to Mom and Dad's tomorrow with me. I didn't think I'd see you today."

He walked past her and turned, holding a newspaper up for her to see. "I wasn't expecting my sister to be on Page Six of the *Post* making out with a man she knows better than to get involved with."

Rena closed the door with a resigned sigh. "It was just a kiss. Everyone was taking pictures of us and I guess I wanted to give them something to photograph."

Kane slammed the paper down on the shelf behind him. "So being with a half-naked man in public wasn't enough to ensure press coverage? You had to seal the deal with your display?"

Rena picked up the paper and studied the photo. "What are you really upset about, Kane? My face is hidden and they didn't list my name. No one will know it's me."

"I know."

Rena dropped the paper and folded her arms in front of her chest. "I get that you're here because you care, Kane, but honestly there is nothing going on between Nick and me. I went to see him last night because I knew he'd gotten into an argument with Gio. We talked. He told me to mind my own business. I got offended and walked away. He followed me to apologize. That's it. That's all that happened."

Kane frowned down at her. "That doesn't explain why he was in his underwear."

Rena hated lying to her brother so she stuck to the truth in her story. "I don't know why Nick does half of what he does. I found him that way. I assumed it was because he'd been with someone upstairs at the club earlier. You'd have to ask him."

Kane's eyes narrowed. "So, nothing happened between the two of you."

"We talked." And kissed, but Rena wasn't about to stoke the fire with that admission.

Not ready to relent, Kane said. "I don't understand the kiss, then."

Rena forced a casual shrug. "It was Nick. We were being photographed. I thought it would be funny."

"I didn't laugh when I saw it," Kane drawled. "Luckily, you're right—most people wouldn't recognize you. No one would expect you to be there in the first place, so this might blow over."

They were both quiet for a moment before Rena said, "Kane, would it be so awful if I did like Nick? We're both adults. What harm could come from it?"

Kane's nostrils flared and a muscle in his jaw clenched. "Stay away from him. You are to have nothing further to do with him. Do you understand?"

Putting her hands on both hips, Rena faced her brother. "You realize I'm not a child anymore, right? I am perfectly capable of making decisions for myself."

Kane growled, "Are you? Nick is everything I hope you're smart enough to avoid. He considers work a disease. He has no respect for women or their marital state. He's a player, and players don't change. Stay away from him."

Rena sighed and let her arms drop to her sides. "You've made your point. Can we drop it now?"

After studying her face for a moment more, Kane's expression softened. "I will as long as you're sure nothing is going on between you and Nick."

Linking her arm with her brother's, Rena said, "I'm done talking about this. I will, however, make you breakfast if you're hungry."

Kane reluctantly let her lead him to the kitchen. "Pancakes?"

Rena smiled. "If you want. Or I could make French toast like our old cook Millie used to make. Do you remember? She taught me the recipe before she retired."

"Since when did you start cooking?" Kane asked as he took a seat at the kitchen counter.

Rena chuckled again and pointed at her head, then down at her toes. "Not twelve anymore, Kane. I've been doing all my own cooking and cleaning since I bought this home. You're just always too busy to realize it."

"Why don't you have staff? You know Mom and Dad would happily pay for them. Hell, I can have my secretary hire someone by tomorrow if you're interested."

Rena opened the door to her refrigerator and started hunting for the necessary ingredients. "Kane, I don't need a maid or a cook. I'm happy just the way I am. I've built a good life for myself and I'm proud to be paying my own way. Mom and Dad raised us to be responsible and independent. And I am. Now can you stop worrying about me? I'm fine."

Kane made a noncommittal sound deep in his throat. "I hope you're being honest with me."

Rena swung back from the stove with a spatula in her hand. "Do you want to eat your breakfast or wear it?"

Kane chuckled. "I'd prefer to eat it."

"That's what I thought," Rena said, not yet lowering her kitchen utensil. "Hey, you didn't say anything to Gio, did you?"

"Not yet, but that doesn't mean he hasn't seen the paper. Or that no one else will bring it to his attention. If I recognized you, others might."

"Kane, what I did last night was impulsive and stupid. I don't want that to make things worse between Nick and Gio—especially when they're already arguing. Promise me you won't say anything to him."

"I may eventually have to tell Gio. If I find out Nick is messing around with you, I'll have to explain to Gio why I killed his brother."

Rena closed her eyes and shook her head. Luckily she had no intention of seeking out Nick again. Impulsive and stupid. That's what she'd told Kane last night was—and it was an accurate description.

Along with—unrepeatable.

Rena raised a hand to touch her lips lightly.

And—unforgettable.

❦

Monday morning, with a towel draped loosely around his hips, Nick bypassed the casual attire hung in his hotel closet and chose a dark blue Gucci suit. He was more than a little surprised the suit had traveled with him from the last hotel he'd stayed in. He didn't have much as far as actual belongings went, which worked out well since he preferred to stay in hotels rather than rent or buy an apartment. He'd always considered both unnecessary commitments.

Without so much as a goldfish to care for, he'd been free to go skiing in the Alps one week and bum around in Bali the next.

Money made a good personal assistant. Enough of it and anything was possible.

Well, not anything. He couldn't say it had ever made him happy.

Or like who he saw staring back at him as he brushed his teeth each morning.

He adjusted the collar of his shirt over a tie and studied his reflection. He looked tired. Not surprising, since he'd hardly slept at all that weekend. He hadn't gone out or answered his phone once.

He'd needed to think a few things through and, although he normally found peace in the chaos of a nightclub, he'd spent the weekend with something more chaotic—himself.

And his desire to see Rena again.

He'd almost called her the next morning, after he'd spent the night reliving how eagerly she'd kissed him up in his VIP balcony. To know she was as attracted to him as he'd always been to her was a heady temptation.

And he'd never been one to deny himself pleasure.

He didn't call her, though, and he couldn't fully understand why. Something in him had changed when he'd told her he'd stopped drinking. She'd been genuinely proud of him. Although their kiss upstairs had been more sexually intense, the kiss they'd shared near the bar was the one that haunted him the most.

He wanted to recapture that moment. More than anything else, he wanted her to look at him that way again.

Why do I care what she thinks of me?

Would fucking her end this obsession?

He turned away from the mirror and shrugged on his suit jacket. That weekend he'd asked himself a plethora of questions that didn't have ready answers, yet he'd come to some decisions.

Rena had said he hadn't given Gio a chance to explain himself. He'd replayed his conversation with his brother a hundred times in his head. Gio claimed to want Nick to be a part of the family company. He'd brought up that damn office that he'd kept open and staffed for him.

Gio and their mother had opposing versions of many subjects. Someone wasn't being honest.

Nick decided he could either deal with this as he always had—by flying off to hang out with his friends and numbing himself past caring, or he could get to the truth for once. Unfortunately, in his family, that wouldn't happen by asking anyone. He'd have to uncover it for himself.

The driver Nick had hired for the day called upstairs to announce his arrival. Nick strode out of his suite with growing determination. By the time he was seated in the back of the town car, he was confident his plan would work.

A short while later, Nick walked into his office. A short, blonde woman in her early twenties stood when he entered. She was attractive enough that if he'd met her months ago, Nick would have asked her for her phone number. Today, he wasn't interested.

"I'm sorry, Mr. Andrade is in a meeting this morning."

Nick cocked his head to one side and raised an eyebrow. "You mean Gio?"

The woman reached for the pencil that was tucked behind one of her ears but dropped it. As she scrambled to pick it up off the floor, she smiled and said, "Oh, you're here to see that Mr. Andrade? He's one floor up. Take a left out of the elevator. His office is right there."

"I know where his office is. I'm not lost."

"Then you're here to see Nicholas Andrade?" She looked at the closed door behind her, then quickly turned back. "He's going to be busy for a while, can I take a message?" She held her pen poised above a notepad.

"What's your name?" Nick asked impatiently.

"Janet."

"How long have you worked here?"

Suddenly flustered, Janet replied, "Three months? I'm sorry. Should I know you? Mr. Andrade doesn't have many people drop by his office."

Nick rubbed his forehead, fighting off a growing headache. "*I'm* Nicholas Andrade."

"Oh," she said and dropped her pencil again. "Really?"

Nick grimaced. "Really."

"Wow, they told me I'd probably never meet you."

Nick heard the irritation in his own voice as he asked, "Who said that?"

"Human resources?" she answered with growing panic in her voice. "I shouldn't have said that. Please don't fire me. I just graduated from college and this is the first job I can put on my résumé that doesn't include serving hamburgers."

"I'm not going to fire you. I don't even know what the hell you do yet."

Janet splayed her hands on the desk in front of her. "I mostly lie about where you are. Usually you're in a meeting. Other times you're traveling to inspect a new site. I try to be creative."

"That's the extent of your job?"

She blushed. "I also input data from departments that need help. Sometimes I cover for someone who is on vacation."

"Janet, call down to HR and tell them your services will no longer be available to them."

"Because I'm fired?"

"No, because your boss is finally out of his meeting."

An hour later the door to Nick's office flew open and his older brother stormed in. "What the hell are you doing, Nick?"

Nick had been asking himself that for the last fifty-nine minutes, but he didn't like hearing the question coming from his brother. "You're the one who said I was a full partner. Isn't this the office you told me was waiting for me?"

Gio walked up to his desk aggressively. "I don't have time for this bullshit, Nick. I don't care why you're in here pretending to be doing something. I want to know what this is." He threw a newspaper down in front of him.

"It's a newspaper," Nick answered drolly. "People used to read it before the Internet."

With a growl, Gio pointed to a photo in the middle of the page. "You know damned well what I'm talking about."

Nick looked down at the paper and saw the photo of him, mostly unclothed, kissing Rena. "Not one of my finer moments."

"Is that Rena?" Gio barked.

Nick stood. "You know it is or you wouldn't be here."

"I told you to stay the hell away from her."

"And I told you that whatever happened or didn't happen between the two of us would never be any of your business."

Gio reached over and grabbed Nick by the collar of his shirt.

Nick grabbed Gio's arm with equal force.

"Don't do something you'll regret, Nick."

"Get your hand off me, Gio."

Gio released him roughly. Nick did the same.

"I don't know what to do with you, Nick," Gio growled, pacing in front of him.

"Try trusting me for once," Nick answered, folding his arms across his chest. "I have no intention of hurting Rena."

With an angry shake of his head, Gio said, "That's the problem. You never *mean* to do anything. Nothing is ever your fault or responsibility." He looked Nick over critically. "Did Mother send you? Is that why you're in a suit?"

"No. I decided on my own it was time to get involved."

"What the fuck are you doing, Nick?"

"Right now?" Nick sat back down at his desk. "Taking my place beside you at Cogent. Isn't this what you always wanted?"

Without saying another word, Gio turned and walked out.

A few minutes later there was a knock on his door. Nick looked up at the ceiling of his office and said, "Come in."

Janet had a notebook and pencil in hand. "Now that you're here, I thought I should ask you what you'd like me to do."

Nick covered his eyes with one hand, then rubbed his eyebrows, trying—unsuccessfully—to stem the pounding behind them. "How good are you at psychoanalysis? Gio's right, I'm sitting in here pretending I know what the fuck I'm doing, telling myself that if I try I can unravel decades of lies. For what? Because I wish I were closer to my brothers? Because I care what Rena thinks of me?" He looked across the room at the woman who was hovering in the doorway. "Where do I go from here?"

Janet turned on her heel and disappeared for a moment. When she returned it was with a stack of pink papers. She walked over and laid them on Nick's desk. "I've been taking messages from people for three months. Here is their contact information and the reasons they called. Maybe you could start there."

Nick flipped through the ridiculously large stack of notes. Everything was there, just as she'd said. At a loss for what else to say, he said, "Thank you, Janet."

She nodded, then stopped just before walking out the door. "My brother died while serving an overseas tour. I miss him so much. If I thought I could see him again, even for a few minutes, I would call every number in that pile. Wanting to be closer to your brothers is nothing to be ashamed of."

Nick nodded.

His cell phone rang and he instinctively answered it. "Hello?"

"Nick, it's Luke. Gio said you're at the office. Mind if I drop by?"

Janet closed the door behind her and Nick picked up one of the papers in front of him. "I'm busy this morning, but I'll have time after five."

"Dinner?"

"Sounds like a plan."

Or at least part of one.

Chapter Five

RENA PUSHED HER chair behind her desk and retrieved her purse from the desk's bottom drawer. For once, she was glad to be going home. Gio was in an awful mood, and although he hadn't said anything to her, she had a pretty good idea why. He'd stopped by her desk a couple of times, glared at her, and looked about to say something, only to storm back into his office. She was tempted to bring up the photo herself, but she doubted it would make the situation better.

Plus, she was already angry enough with herself—she didn't need to endure what most likely would be another lecture. She knew she shouldn't have gone to see Nick at the club. She absolutely shouldn't have kissed him on the balcony. There was no rational explanation for why she'd kissed him again in front of the bar when she knew they were being photographed. And if that wasn't bad enough, she'd waited all weekend for Nick to contact her.

And, of course, he hadn't.

Because a man like Nick wouldn't. He'd probably left the club to continue his hookup with whoever he'd gotten undressed for.

I'm such an idiot.

Rena had gone to her parents' house for dinner that weekend, and although Kane had been there, he hadn't mentioned Nick again. He hadn't needed to. By that time, Rena had worked through her initial disappointment at not hearing from Nick and compiled a mental list of every reason why his lack of interest was for the best.

She'd worked at hardening her heart against the problems that lay between Nick and Gio. Kane was right: It was none of her business.

Her phone vibrated, announcing a text message. Rena retrieved it from the bottom of her purse as she headed out the door.

I've been warned to stay away from you—Nick.

Rena stopped dead. Her heart beat crazily in her chest. She typed back, **Me too**.

Is Gio giving you a hard time about the photo? I'll talk to him.

Unwelcomed warmth spread through Rena as she read his words. She'd built up a strong wall of defense against his charm. She answered, **Not necessary. My warning came from Kane.**

Want me to explain it to him?

Rena bit back a smile as she imagined how well that would go over with her brother. **I already did. Please don't say anything else to him. It'll make it worse.**

There was no response for long enough that Rena replaced her phone and started walking toward the elevator. She paused when she felt her phone vibrate again.

I have a problem.

Just one? Rena typed back, unable to resist the tongue-in-cheek retort.

I don't want to stay away from you.

"Going home already?" Gio's voice boomed from the door of Rena's office.

She jumped and dropped her phone. She quickly retrieved it and turned to face her boss.

"It's six o'clock."

Gio frowned at her. "I wasn't critiquing your work ethics, but I want to talk to you before you leave."

Rena's phone vibrated in her hand, but she didn't look down at it. "I can't today, Gio. I have somewhere I need to be." *It's called Anywhere but Here.*

"This will only take a minute."

Her phone vibrated again.

"Can we talk tomorrow, Gio? I really do have to go."

The elevator door opened behind Rena and she breathed a sigh of relief when Gio's fiancée walked out of it. She'd feared it would be Nick. She'd never been so happy to see Julia Bennett.

Julia greeted Rena, walked over to Gio, gave him a sweet quick kiss of greeting, then looked back and forth between the two as she sensed the tension between them. "What's going on?"

Gio hugged Julia and said, "Good. You're here. You're better at this than I am."

"Better at what?" Julia asked, once again studying them.

"Gio's upset because I kissed Nick," Rena said, hoping to diffuse the tension by making light of the incident. "It was a joke, which unfortunately made it into some local rag. My fault. I thought it would be funny."

Julia clapped her hands together. "So, it was you. I knew it. I recognized the outfit." She smiled. "A hazard of my security training. I can't turn it off."

"I was hoping you were wrong, Julia, but Nick confirmed it this morning," Gio said, clearly still unhappy with the situation.

A vibration announced yet another text message. Rena glanced down at her phone to make sure Nick wasn't on his way to see her.

All I can think about is kissing you again.

And more. Much much more.

Meet me tonight.

Rena flushed at the memory of how easily she'd almost said yes to him already. She stuffed her phone deep in her purse.

Julia took Gio's hand in hers. "Even if it wasn't a joke, what would be so bad about Rena dating Nick? She might be a good influence on him."

Gio looked around the hallway. "This isn't the appropriate place for this discussion. Let's go back into the office for a minute."

Wow, sounds tempting, but no. "Gio, I love you, but what you're not understanding is that I don't want to talk about this anymore. I already went through the whole thing on Saturday with Kane. I'm done. I did it. It was stupid. I'm sorry. Can we drop it?"

"I wish I could, but—"

Julia interrupted him, "Gio, don't."

"She needs to know the truth about Nick."

A sad expression darkened Julia's face. "Are you sure you know the truth? Maybe you should try talking to him again."

"I did. He's angry and he's messing with the only two things he knows will bother me: Rena and Cogent," Gio said angrily. "You heard him yourself, Rena. He's following through on what he threatened. He's going to fuck with Cogent. And he'll use you to help him if you let him."

"I don't believe you," Rena said, shaking her head. "Nick isn't the vengeful type."

"Then, tell me, why did he spend the day in his office today? He's calling contacts, pretending he actually works here. I don't know what he's up to, but I will stop him."

Julia took one of his hands in both of hers. "Gio, you scare me when you talk like this. He's your brother."

Gio's face softened when he looked down into his fiancée's eyes. "I'm sorry, Jules. I wish I could protect you from this, but you also need to know who you can trust. In my family, the one who will cut you the deepest is the one who pretends to care the most."

Julia turned to Rena. "I wish I knew what to say. I don't want to believe anyone is capable of behaving that way, but I also know that Gio loves Nick. If he's warning you to stay away from him, he probably has a very good reason."

Deep in her purse, Rena closed her hand over her phone. "I heard Nick's threat, Gio, but I also heard you tell him that you'd kept an office for him all this time. Maybe this is his attempt to make things right with you."

"Do you honestly believe that?" Gio asked, a thick layer of skepticism coating his voice.

I want to.

Rena took a deep breath and fought back her own emotional response to Gio's accusations. It was one thing to be another potential notch on Nick's bedpost, and quite another to be a pawn in a feud with his family. *Bottom line: Nothing really happened between us, and nothing ever will.*

Some of this is my fault for forgetting why I went to see him in the first place. I wanted to help Nick and Gio heal, not give them another reason to rip each other apart.

With that in mind, Rena looked Gio in the eye. "I don't know why Nick is working here, but he would never intentionally hurt you or me. You can say you spoke to Nick, but the two of you don't talk *to* each other—you talk *at* each other. Until you stop and actually listen to him, you'll never know why he's here. And Nick will never explain himself as long as he thinks you won't believe him. So, go to it. Defend your precious family company against the very people you say you built it for. Push Nick until he does what you expect him to, but don't think you're not equally to blame for what happens."

Gio's face twisted with regret. "This morning when I asked him what he wanted, he said he wanted me to trust him for once."

Julia hugged Gio's side. "Maybe you should. You said things were different with your brothers when you all came back from Stephan's wedding. Maybe Rena's right and he's trying to reach out to you."

With a pained expression, Gio looked across at Rena. "I would do anything for my brothers—you know that. I want to trust Nick."

"Then give him a chance to prove himself." As Gio softened to the idea, Rena prayed she was right. *Please, Nick. Please be here because you want to patch things up with your family. This is your chance. Get it right this time.*

"The photograph was honestly your doing? There isn't anything going on between you and Nick?" Rena knew her answer would determine how much he would or wouldn't trust his brother's intentions.

So she forced a smile. "Nick and I have always ribbed each other, but it's always been just that—a joke. I had no idea he'd decided to work here, because we're not close. I went to see him because I felt badly about how the two of you had argued. He was at that club he frequents. I should have left him alone, but I thought I could help. I'm sorry my little prank at the end of that visit caused anyone worry. That wasn't my intention."

Julia's easy smile returned. "See, Gio, it's not as bad as you thought. Let's go home. You can talk to Nick tomorrow after you've both had a day to cool down."

Gio nodded. "That's a good idea." With his arm around Julia, he said, "Rena, sorry about my mood today." He gave her a small smile. "I'll think about what you said. You've known us for a long time. I should tell you to stay out of this, but God knows my family is in need of an intervention. I almost strangled Nick this morning. You don't know how relieved I am to hear he's not messing with you. When I saw that photo, I thought for sure he was."

Rena let out a long breath. "Don't kill your brother. This time it was me," she said, forcing a light tone into her voice.

Arm in arm, Gio and Julia walked away, talking in a tone that made their words inaudible. They entered the elevator and held the door. Julia asked, "Rena, are you coming?"

Shaking her head, Rena said, "Not yet. I forgot something in my desk. Go on without me."

The door closed on them, and Rena brought a shaky hand to her temple. With her other hand she retrieved her phone and reread Nick's messages.

He wanted to see her.

And more.

Rena shivered as she imagined all the possible things that could mean. Images of the two of them, naked and sprawled across his bed, sweaty from a marathon of raw fucking, brought a blush to Rena's cheeks. Part of her wanted to simply text **Yes.**

Yes to whatever he had in mind. If their kiss was anything to go by, sex with Nick would be unlike anything she'd experienced.

It wouldn't be warm and comfortable.

It would be hot, consuming... and wrong.

The heat of the desire that throbbed through her was cooled by the doubt Gio had planted in her heart. Would Nick use her to get back at Gio? Would he sleep with her to get information about Cogent that he could use to take Gio down?

She didn't want to believe he was capable of it, but she wasn't sure anymore.

She read his texts again.

Nick has never lied to me. He doesn't lie. That's part of how he always gets in trouble. He says it as it is. No, he argued with Gio because he was worried about his mother. He threatened Gio because he wanted to make a point. He kissed me because...

Okay, it's better not to think about why he kissed me and just focus on why it can't happen again. Even if his interest in her were sincere, being with Nick would only hurt his chances of making up with Gio. Giving in to temptation would achieve the exact opposite of what she'd hoped to achieve by going to see him.

Whether you're asking me out because you're trying to stick it to your brother, Nick, or because you found our kiss as amazing as I did—my answer has to be the same.

She chose her path and typed, **I'm sorry, Nick. I don't feel that way about you. We're friends. Nothing more.**

He didn't text back.

Cʒ

Nick threw his phone on his desk and slumped forward, his head in his hands. He'd told himself not to text Rena. He'd spent the day fighting off the desire to go upstairs and see her.

He didn't believe for a moment she wasn't interested in him. No woman kisses a man the way she'd kissed him unless she feels something for him.

She's scared. She said she'd been warned to stay away from him, and Rena had always been one to play it safe.

He told himself he should respect her decision.

He should call any of the women he'd been with recently and fuck them until he couldn't remember how incredibly hot Rena's mouth had been. Or how her tight little body had felt pressed against him. He needed to do something that would dull how vividly he remembered how her perfectly rounded ass felt in his hands.

There was only one reason he wouldn't do that.

He looked down at his traitorous dick. "You've never been picky before. Why start now?"

"Who are you talking to?" his brother Luke asked from the doorway. "I didn't see your secretary at her desk—tell me she's not under yours. That's not a good start to working here."

Nick stood, shaking his head with reluctant amusement at being caught talking to his cock. "I'm alone."

Luke didn't look convinced.

Nick waved at the area below his desk. "You can check if you don't believe me."

Janet popped her head in behind Luke. "Mr. Andrade, I'm so sorry. I went down to HR like you asked me to. I probably shouldn't have left my desk. I guess I'm still getting used to you being here." She looked from Luke to Nick and then hastily added, "Not that you're not always here and haven't always been here. Because you have been. Right here. In your office. Every day."

Nick raised a hand to stop her. "Relax, Janet. This is my brother Luke."

A smile returned to her face. "Thank God. Hey, then do you mind if I go home now? I actually worked today."

Nick couldn't help but smile back. He had the secretary he deserved, he supposed. He shrugged. At least he'd never wonder what she was thinking. "Go home. I'm done for the day. See you tomorrow."

"Really?" she asked, sounding pleased.

"Totally," he answered with humor, but she didn't get the joke. Being around her made him feel old.

Luke dropped into the chair in front of Nick's desk. "Well, she's pretty. Not that I'd expect you to have anything different, but you might want to find yourself a secretary that sounds like she's out of high school."

"I don't care how she looks or how she sounds, as long as she does her job."

Folding his arms across his chest, Luke sat back and studied Nick. "You mean that."

"Is that so hard to believe?"

Luke cocked his head to one side. "A little. So it's true— you're working here. Why the sudden interest in Cogent?"

"You're the one who kept encouraging me to give it a second try."

Sitting forward in his chair, Luke said, "You don't have to prove anything to me, Nick. I'm on your side. What are you really doing here?"

Nick walked around his desk and sat in the chair across from his brother. "Did you ever get the feeling that things aren't the way they're supposed to be? When we were on Isola Santos Uncle Victor gave a long speech."

"I remember."

"He kept saying the most important things to any Andrade are family and taking care of the next generation. Father didn't take care of us very well. We don't take care of each other. Hell, if it weren't for you, I doubt Gio, Max, and I would speak outside of the holidays. I wanted to be the kind of Andrade Uncle Victor described. I started spending more time with Mother, and it all went to shit after that." Nick leaned forward, resting his elbows on his knees. "She has a way of making me doubt which way the sun comes up. I can't tell if she's lying or if Gio is. Every time I try to figure it out I discover another reason to be angry. Last year I would have thrown my hands up and walked away. I don't want to do that this time. This time, I want the truth."

"About?"

"About any of it—all of it. Why did Mother want to keep us away from Father's side of the family? Why didn't Gio tell us we had a half sister?" Nick stopped and watched Luke's expression. "How long have *you* known about Gigi?"

"Gio told me about her after he found out you knew."

"And that didn't make you fucking nuts? That he knew something that important and didn't tell us?"

Luke balled one hand into fist. "I have to believe that he thought he was doing what was best for all of us. He said he intended to tell us before Mother's episode."

"He said he only found out when we went to Stephan's wedding. You believe that, too?"

"I do."

"Why?"

"Because that's what he told me, and Gio is many things but he's not a liar." The two brothers sat in silence for a long time, then Luke said, "I don't know what happened between Mother and our uncles. Or why Father needed another family in Venice when he had us. Whatever happened has weighed heavily on Mother for a long time. You were right to spend time with her. She's very unhappy right now."

"Because of her heart attack."

Luke sighed. "If she had one."

"Are you suggesting that she didn't?" Nick's head snapped back.

"I'm not suggesting anything. Listen, Gio and Mother are at odds, and that's never good for any of us. They both have a hard time letting go of the past. What's the truth and what's a lie? I don't know. But does it matter? Would knowing change anything? Let it go."

"Well, Ghandi, you're a better person than I am. I can't let it go. I'm done walking away. I'm going to work here, side by side with Gio, until I get some answers."

Luke nodded.

Nick's eyebrows shot up in surprise. "You're not going to tell me that I don't belong here? Warn me to leave now before the wrath of Gio descends upon me?"

"No, I think you're where you need to be."

"That wasn't at all what I expected you to say."

Luke stood and for once his smile didn't reach his eyes. "None of us are the Andrades we thought we'd grow up to be. I want to know the truth, too." He laid a hand on Nick's shoulder. "Gio kept this office for you because he always believed you belonged here. He may not tell you that he loves you, but this is proof that he does. Remember that while you search for your answers." He dropped his hand. "Now, let's go to dinner and talk about all the reasons you had better not be dating Rena."

Nick stood and chuckled. "You're making me sorry I gave up drinking."

Luke's eyes widened in surprise. "Did you really?"

"Three months sober."

Luke gave him a pat on the back and a wide grin spread across his face, this time brightening his eyes. "Now that is something worth celebrating. Come on, let's get out of here."

As they walked out, Luke said, "You should tell Gio. He'd be happy for you, too."

Nick shrugged. "I'm sure he'll know, now that you do."

The both turned when they entered the elevator and stood shoulder to shoulder. Without looking at Nick, Luke said, "No, this time I'm staying out of it. You and Gio need to work out your issues. On your terms. Not mine."

"You? Stay out of it? That's like telling Rena to mind her own business."

"Oh, yes, back to Rena. What is going on there?"

"We're friends," Nick said and made a face as he did. "Nothing more."

Chapter Six

TWO WEEKS LATER, Rena was sitting at her desk reviewing the calendar on her computer when her cell phone rang. Gio was out of the office for the morning, so she answered it without hesitation.

As soon as she heard the voice that greeted her, she wished she'd taken the time to check caller ID.

"Rena," the woman said cheerfully.

"Maddy, what a surprise. If you're looking for Gio, he's out of the office this morning."

"Actually, I'm calling to talk to you. It's a private matter. Do you have a moment?"

"It's pretty busy here today. Could I call you—"

"This will be quick. I promise. I heard that Nick is working there now. Is that true?"

Rena pushed a pen around on her desk. "I never feel comfortable discussing Cogent business with anyone."

"I'm not just anyone, I'm their cousin. Besides, I couldn't care less about the business side of why he's there. Have you met his secretary?"

"I've spoken to her on the phone."

"Does she seem to like her job more now that Nick is there?"

Rena picked up the pen and started to doodle on a piece of paper. "I haven't spoken to her enough to know."

"Could you? Speak to her, I mean. It would look weird if I started hanging around Nick's office, but I have to know how they are getting along. Curiosity is killing me. Luke told me Nick likes her, but he won't say more than that."

Rena pressed so hard on the pen that it tore into the paper. She threw the pen down. "I don't understand."

Maddy said excitedly, "Don't you think she would be perfect for Nick? She comes from a great family in Connecticut. And she's drop-dead gorgeous."

"Janet is one of your plants?"

"Not mine, but I don't care. She applied for a job at Corisi Enterprises. Marie interviewed her and snapped her up, then we pulled a few strings and sent her over to Cogent. Don't worry, Marie did a full background check on her and her family. Her mother is an elementary school teacher. Her father works as a hospital administrator. Janet put herself through school by working at a fast-food chain. Everyone there loved her. They all say she has a heart of gold. That's exactly the kind of woman Nick needs. Someone who can love him unconditionally."

"Who is Marie?"

"Mrs. Duhamel, Dominic Corisi's personal assistant. She practically runs his company. I can't believe you don't know her. You would love her. Just don't mess with her boys. She's very protective of them."

"Maddy, as interesting as this is, I have to get back to work." And try to forget that Nick likely took her brush-off so well because he'd already moved on to sleeping with his secretary.

"Don't hang up. Rena, I know you said you don't want to get involved, but all you'd have to do is peek in and see how they are together. Janet doesn't know she's a plant so she won't know why you're there. That's it. Maybe put in a good word for him to her. Or vice versa. Nothing more than that."

Rena looked up at the ceiling. *Does someone up there hate me?* "I'm sorry, Maddy, I told you. This isn't something I want to be a part of."

"I get it. You have to be discrete. That's fine. Keep it simple. I'll call you tomorrow."

Rena sighed after Maddy hung up. Speaking to her was always a little bit like stepping into a hurricane: You had to fight to keep your footing. Nicole had been right—Maddy definitely had a problem with the word *no*.

A few minutes later, Rena was still gathering her thoughts when Nick walked into her office. She should be used to seeing him in a suit and tie, but the sight still took her breath away. No matter how many times he came up to see Gio, Rena's response to him was the same. Her heart beat triple-time and her hands itched to reach out and mess his recently tamed hair.

"Is Gio in?"

"He stepped out for a meeting."

"Do you know when he'll be back?"

"He didn't say."

Rena cursed herself for being angry at Nick for respecting her wish to ignore what had happened between them. He had been completely businesslike each time they'd met since and it made her more confused.

It was probably easy for him since he likely consoled himself in the arms of his secretary.

Bastard.

Rena knew she should be happy that Gio and Nick had come to something of a truce. Nick had come by to talk to Gio almost every day recently, and it looked like Gio was trusting him with more and more responsibility. Gio had even mentioned that he was impressed with how Nick was both coming to him for guidance and bringing his own ideas. If all went well, the two would indeed end up as partners. Nick was surprising everyone.

And looking so damn pleased with himself I want to throw a shoe at his head.

He walked over to the side of her desk and laid one hand down flat, bringing his mouth close enough that he could speak softly in her ear. "I can't tell if you're angry with me because I kissed you that night or because I haven't kissed you since."

Rena kept her eyes glued to her keyboard. "I'm not angry at all."

"Is that why you glare at me every time I come in here? I won't apologize for what I said to you afterward." He lowered his voice to a whisper. "You're not fooling me, Rena. I know you enjoyed that kiss as much as I did. The thought of repeating it is keeping me up at night. Just being in the same room with you makes me painfully hard. I want to fuck you, Rena. It's going to happen. How long can you hold out, pretending you don't want it as much as I do?"

In a voice much more breathy and excited than she'd intended, Rena answered, "I'm not pretending."

"Look me in the eye and say that, Rena."

She couldn't. If she turned her head she wasn't sure she could stop her lips from seeking his. "I—"

Her denial was cut off by Gio entering her office. "Nick, you're here. Good. I wanted to update you on our newest client."

Nick straightened. "Great. Did you mention the stats I gave you?"

"I did and they were a nice touch. Good thinking. Rena, hold my calls for the next thirty minutes."

"Absolutely," Rena said, striving to sound unaffected by her exchange with Nick.

Nick followed Gio, but just before he stepped into Gio's office, he turned and winked at Rena. A deep red flush spread up her neck and face.

She glared at him.

He smiled back at her and closed the door behind him. Rena laid her head on her desk and groaned audibly.

"Is this a bad time?" a woman asked tentatively.

Rena rolled her head to one side and peered at the woman with one eye. She was in her mid-twenties, with long blonde curls that hung wildly around a heart-shaped face and stunning green eyes. If the tiny waist and huge breasts were anything to go by, she had to be Janet.

"No," Rena answered as she raised her head. "I was reading over some notes."

The woman glanced down at the empty desk in front of Rena, then shrugged. "Hi, I'm Janet Wagner. We've spoken on the phone a few times. I'm Nicholas Andrade's secretary. Do you have a minute?"

With a sigh of resignation, Rena sat back in her chair, "Sure. What do you need?"

The young woman stepped closer to Rena's desk. "Nick asked me to type up some summary notes. I did, but I don't know if they need to be in a certain format. Could you look at what I did and tell me if you think that's what he wants?"

I know what he wants, Rena thought but didn't say. *And the problem is: I want the same thing.*

Rena stood and pushed past Janet. "I'm sorry. I can't do this right now." She kept walking until she was in the privacy of the bathroom. Once inside she locked the outer door and stood in front of the sink facing her reflection. *Don't sleep with him. Everything is finally going well for him. Gio is beginning to trust him. He's actually finding his way here.*

Fucking him could seriously fuck that up.

Fuck. Look at what I'm becoming.

I don't even swear normally.

This is not good.

Pull yourself together.

A glint of satisfaction lit her eyes. *He wants me.*

She closed her eyes and shook her head.

But that doesn't change anything.

She opened her eyes, reminded herself that she was not the type to hide in a bathroom instead of conquering a challenge, and told herself to go help Janet with her summary.

I can do this because I know I made the right decision for Nick and for me.

If he wants to fuck her it's none of my business.

Fuck, I'm swearing again.

She took a deep breath and unlocked the bathroom door. She looked up at the ceiling and said, "I don't know who I pissed off up there, but could you work with me? Just a little? I'm trying to do the right thing here."

❦

Nick sat in one of the leather chairs in front of Gio's desk. He forced himself into a relaxed pose. Gio hovered beside his desk. For the past two weeks he'd looked down at him from his desk chair like a king tolerating one of his subjects. Something had changed.

"The meeting went well this morning. You were spot-on with how Durkin would respond to our counteroffer. How did you know that?"

"I spent a week at his house in Bali last year. Durkin Senior likes to talk when he drinks. At the time I found it tediously boring, but he bragged extensively about the equipment his company was developing. Sounded like a large investment project. Which implied a possible cash flow issue until they prove their new design works. Two months ago we received a call from one of his people. They were feeling out what our next contracts would be. I figured they were ripe for a lowball offer from us."

"You figured right." Gio surprised Nick by sitting down across from him. He cleared his throat. "That deal will make a substantial difference in the profit margin. You did good."

Nick tensed at the praise. His family knew exactly how to soften someone up before cutting them down. He and Gio hadn't spoken about anything personal since he'd returned to Cogent, but it appeared that was about to change. "And?"

Gio ran a hand through his hair. "I'm sorry."

Nick sat forward. "What? You obviously have something you want to say to me."

Gio looked at him silently for a long moment. "I didn't know what to do when Father died. I was angry with him when I discovered his mistress in Venice. At that time, I didn't know about Gigi. I swear, Nick, that wouldn't have been a secret I would have kept."

"Why did you keep any? Didn't I have a right to know the truth?"

"I thought I was protecting the family. I was wrong." Gio punched his thigh in frustration. "I was wrong about a lot of things. Mother was devastated by the revelation that Father had another family. That was followed by a realization that he hadn't been honest with anyone about the state of the company. Cogent was sinking. We were one contract away from closing our doors. I remember feeling like everything was spinning out of control. I thought if I could get Cogent back on track everything else would return to normal. I didn't want you to know how bad things were. I see now that by keeping you out of the loop I blocked you from becoming an effective team member."

"You sound like you're making a deathbed confession. I don't buy it."

Gio accepted that with a nod. "I don't expect you to trust me immediately. I thought the worst of you when you were determined to work here. Luke said you're here seeking the truth. I don't have all of the answers you're looking for, but I have some. Whatever Mother has against Victor and Alessandro, it has something to do with Isola Santos."

"Our family's private island?"

"Yes. It should have gone to me, but Mother made sure it didn't. She gave the deed for it back to our uncles and lied about it."

"Do you have proof of that?"

"Victor told me the deed had been in Mother's possession before Father died. Which made sense since it always goes to the oldest male child in the family."

"The uncles have lied about many things over the years. They never accepted her or us."

"I used to believe that, but not anymore. As soon as they knew I was interested in Isola Santos, they offered it to me. No, someone has been lying to us, but I don't believe it was them."

Nick stood and shook his head.

Gio stood also and continued. "None of this is easy for me to say. I love our mother, too. And she is ill, just not in the way she'd like us to believe."

"You've never told me any of this before. Why say it now?"

Gio held out a hand for emphasis. "You and I have been at odds for a long time, but these past two weeks have proven it doesn't have to be that way. We can be on the same team." A sad expression entered his eyes and he lowered his hand. "You don't believe me."

"I didn't say that." Nick sat immobile while his mind raced. Gio seemed forthright, open, and almost earnest in his desire for Nick to believe him. Which either meant what he said was true, or there was something Gio was afraid he would uncover.

Gio went to his desk and returned with a folder. "Take this. It's the Durkin file. I had planned to meet with him and Congressman Blasett next week to facilitate the site testing and formalize the government approval. Why don't you lead that meeting? Rena has all my notes. She can bring you up to speed on everything we've done so far. If you need her, take her with you to his office. She knows all the players involved. This will free me up to check out a potential site in Canada." He held the folder out to Nick. "Are you ready for the challenge?"

Nick took the folder and met Gio's eyes. This wasn't how he'd imagined the morning going at all. "You're asking me to work with Rena? Didn't you warn me to stay away from her?"

Gio laid a hand on Nick's shoulder. "I overreacted to that stupid photo. You've known Rena as long as I have. If something was going to happen between the two of you, it would have happened a long time ago. I should have trusted you."

Nick frowned. Whether or not Gio was being entirely honest with him, Nick wasn't about to lie to him. "Gio, I can't guarantee..."

Misreading what Nick was about to say, Gio gave him a supportive pat on the back. "You'll do fine. Especially if you work with Rena on this. The framework for the deal has already been banged out on all sides. All you have to do is get it in writing."

Nick nodded and left Gio's office with folder in hand. The deal wasn't the part he was worried about.

He stopped in front of Rena's desk and said, "It looks like the two of us will be working together. I'm taking over the Durkin project. I realize tomorrow is Saturday, but I need to get up to speed on it as soon as possible. So, my place or yours?"

Rena's eyes rounded and she licked her bottom lip nervously. "I don't think either is a good idea. How about here?"

Giving in to temptation, Nick leaned down and growled into her ear, "I've pictured fucking you on your desk as many times as I have imagined you in my bed, or in my car, or against your office door. Location is not going to make this any easier." The scent of her perfume was heaven to him. "I know you feel the same."

She didn't deny it. How could she? Her own breathing revealed how his words were affecting her. She pulled her head back so she could meet his eyes. "Then the smart thing to do is to not meet at all. I can send you the information I have. It's easy enough to do this online. We could even FaceTime if you'd like."

"Afraid?" he asked and loved how she shivered at his question.

"No," she denied hotly a second later.

"Good, then meet me."

"Fine," she said and reached for a sticky note. As she spoke, she wrote an address on the paper. "This is the coffee shop around the corner from my house. It has tables where we can sit and talk. Espresso Express. I'll meet you there at ten. By then the rush is over and we can talk without being disturbed." She handed the paper to him primly.

He pocketed the paper. "You always were good at playing it safe."

Her eyes held a mix of heat and defiance. "And you always do whatever you want."

He took her chin in his hand with a less-than-gentle grip. "That's how you see me?"

She broke off their connection with a flip of her chin. "Count me out of whatever game you're playing. I'll work with you because I want you to succeed here, but if you're interested in anything else, call your secretary. Unless you're already sick of tapping that well."

"Tapping that well?" He threw his head back and laughed. "I love it. And you know what else I love? You, jealous. That haughty, dismissive tone is hot." His expression turned more serious. "For the record, I haven't tapped anyone's well for months."

He walked to the door of her office, turned, and put a hand to his throat. "Parched."

She crumpled up a piece of paper and threw it at him. "Get out of here."

He turned around to look at her one more time from the doorway. "Tomorrow at ten."

As he walked away, the confusion he felt while talking to his brother melted away. When it came to family matters, he didn't know who to believe yet. Normally, that would have soured his mood. However, he was about to spend a day with Rena.

He smiled.

They could start with business. In fact, it was important that they did. He needed to be ready for the Durkin meeting the following week.

But after that...

Whatever happens—happens.

Chapter Seven

THE NEXT MORNING, Rena used the short walk to the coffee shop to get her head together. Nick liked to shock people. That's all his suggestive comments yesterday had been about. He wanted to see if he could get under her skin. And he'd succeeded.

Just as he always had.

If she had been looking for confirmation that meeting him was a bad idea, she'd only have to call any of her friends or family. Kane believed Nick wasn't at Cogent for good reasons. Her friends had always considered her crush on him to be one of her few flaws. They called him a narcissistic playboy. Not that that would have stopped any of them from sleeping with him if he'd shown any interest in them.

Which thankfully he hadn't. Rena liked to believe that was out of respect for her.

Despite all of Nick's outrageous flirtations and daredevil stunts, she'd never seen him deliberately hurt anyone. She'd never caught him in a lie or been confused about his motives. He was impulsive, brash, and irreverent when it came to authority. He knew exactly how to get a rise out of someone and wasn't above making sport of it. But she had also seen tenderness in him.

She thought back to her sixteenth birthday party. Her parents had planned it for months. They'd invited their friends and colleagues. Rather than the pool party she'd requested, it was to be a formal event—one she'd vented about in front of Nick and his brothers while they were all on a ski trip. She didn't want tea and flowers; she wanted music and Slip 'N Slides. Kane had explained that she was growing up and that those types of parties were for children. Gio had agreed. Luke had tried to make her see the importance of the landmark birthday from her parents' point of view. Max had bet that complaining wouldn't change anything since the invitations had already been sent out.

Nick hadn't said a word.

On the day of her party, a caravan of trucks had pulled up in their long circular driveway. Before her parents had been able to stop it, an entire petting zoo had begun to unload on their front lawn. The drivers had been adamant they had the right address. Her father had been furious. Her mother had been frantic to get the animals off her lawn before the guests inside saw them.

That chaos had allowed another vehicle to pull up to the rear of the house. Three young men had unloaded speakers and inflated the tallest Slip 'N Slide she'd ever seen, along with a couple of changing tents and an assortment of bathing suits. The petting zoo had been instantly forgotten by her crowd as they'd cheered in surprise and changed into swimwear.

Still in her formal dress, Rena had been both horrified and moved by the gesture. Someone had given her exactly what she'd wanted that day. Although she'd desperately wanted to run outside and join her friends, she'd also been afraid to disappoint her parents. So she'd hung back, frozen by her own sense of right and wrong.

Nick had come to stand beside her as she'd looked out the window at her friends. He'd come back from college for her birthday. That alone was something she'd never forget. But he'd also said, "Don't let anyone guilt you into being someone you're not. This is your chance. Go. Everyone is so angry with me, no one will care if you have a little fun." He'd looked over his shoulder and laughed. "In fact, I believe your father just found me out because he's heading this way and he does not look happy. I'd better go."

She'd caught his arm and asked, "You did this? For me? Why?"

He'd given her a wink that had melted her heart. "It's what you wanted, wasn't it?"

Then he'd wisely bolted before her father had had a chance to corner him. Gio hadn't been as lucky. Rena sighed as she remembered how she'd never changed out of her dress. She'd spent the next hour apologizing to her father and calming her mother. She'd dutifully returned to the tea and endured another hour of her parents' guests while her friends had enjoyed the waterslide.

Even though the party had gone down in her family's history as the event Nick Andrade had ruined, it was on that day that Rena had fallen helplessly and irreversibly in puppy love with him. The gesture had been as brash as Robin Hood's act of rebellion, and as romantic as any made by a fairy-tale prince. She'd spent many nights dreaming of being swept off her feet by Nick.

But childhood fantasies must all eventually be put to rest.

Very few children actually grow up to be the astronauts their parents told them they could be.

And adolescent crushes naturally fall to the wayside for more realistic relationships.

I'm not a princess in a tower waiting to be saved.

I'm a grown woman, perfectly capable of making my own decisions and living a life without regrets.

Except one: I wish I'd been brave enough to join my friends outside instead of doing the right thing.

Which doesn't mean I'm going to sleep with Nick. I haven't completely lost my mind. All I've agreed to is coffee in a busy coffee shop. She glanced down at her outfit. *Okay, and I may have also chosen to wear the short red dress my friends say I look amazing in.*

She stopped.

Oh, shit. I forgot to bring my laptop and notes. Now I'm going to be late.

She turned on her heel, headed back to her town house, and ran up to her office. As she slung her computer bag over her shoulder and closed the door to her home, she lectured herself.

This is a business meeting.

Nothing more.

He'll say something to try to make me blush.

I'll brush it off.

And that'll be it.

Moments later she paused outside the door of Espresso Express to take a few calming breaths. She'd rushed to get there, and she told herself that that was the only reason her heart was beating wildly in her chest.

She frowned when she saw the sign on the door of the shop announcing it was closed. She'd never known it to close, especially not on a weekend morning. Disappointment filled her. Nick had probably come and gone already.

I made myself crazy for nothing.

Just as she was preparing to turn away and call Nick, the door to the shop opened. Nick stood there, dressed casually in jeans and a polo shirt, as if nothing were out of the norm. "Are you coming in?"

Rena hugged her computer bag to her side. "Isn't it closed?"

"For everyone but us."

Rena peered past him into the coffee shop. "You paid them to close for the day?"

A roguish smile spread across his face. "Due to the nature of our meeting I thought a little privacy was warranted."

"Is anyone else in there? The owners? That tall kid who always messes up my bagel orders?"

"They set up and left. Trust me, they didn't mind. I promised them some new espresso machines. And Carl is studying for his exams. He was happy to have the day off with pay."

When someone walked up to see why the shop was closed, Nick pulled her inside and shut the door behind her. He also closed the blinds, leaving the interior dimly lit despite the time of day. "We're finally alone."

Rena folded her arms over her chest. "This wasn't what I had planned at all and you know it."

Nick guided her farther into the shop with a hand on her lower back. "You said it yourself—I do what I want. And I want you, Rena."

Rena froze. He lowered his head and spoke softly in her ear as his hand splayed across her lower back in an almost reassuring caress. "Tell me you're scared." He turned her so she was facing him. "But don't tell me you don't want this as much as I do, because I'd never believe you."

Rena met his eyes angrily and licked her bottom lip. "You're that sure of yourself?"

He followed the path of her tongue with his thumb. "I lay awake at night thinking about how you'd feel beneath me, on top of me, wrapped around me in every way you could be. I want to hear you call out my name when you come. I want to sink into your pussy and pound away until I lose myself inside you. I see the way you look at me. You want it just as badly."

Rena was only partially aware her computer bag was slipping off her shoulder until Nick stopped it from hitting the floor. He placed it on the table beside them and returned his attention to her. "Well, Rena? What's it going to be?"

Images of a younger her, sadly standing in a dress by a window, flickered through Rena's mind. The childhood feelings she'd had for him rushed forward to embrace the mature ache she knew only he could appease.

For once, she didn't want to do the right thing.

She wanted to do the wrong one—again and again, on every table in the shop and every inch of the counter behind them. She took his face between her hands, went up onto her tiptoes, and pulled him down to meet her lips.

With a groan, he gathered her to him, meeting her passion with his own. He ran his hands down her sides and along the outside of her thighs. As they came up, he raised the hem of her dress with them, bunching it around her waist. With two strong hands he cupped her ass and lifted her slightly so he could grind her against his hard cock.

Rena had kissed her share of men, but she'd never experienced anything like this. Nick claimed her mouth with his, thrusting his tongue inside with a confidence and skill. Although she'd initiated the contact, he'd taken the lead and brought an intimacy and heat to the caress that trumped all that had come before.

This was no gentle request. This was a claiming, and one that she was more than willing to give herself to.

His mouth left hers and trailed hot kisses from her ear to her shoulder. His breath tickled, heated, and drove her out of her mind as his hands expertly removed her dress. With a flip it was over her head and she was in his arms in nothing but her panties, bra, and sandals.

With a flick of his wrist, her bra fell to the floor. His mouth closed over one of her nipples, expertly lapping and teasing it as his hand eased her panties down her legs. She stepped out of them, half in a daze of pleasure, while his mouth trailed lower, kissing a path down her body. Every one of his touches sent shivers through her, until his teeth grazed her neatly trimmed sex.

He slowly kissed his way back up to her other breast, and this hot repeat assault had her clinging to his shoulders. This time he suckled between gentle nips and Rena gasped aloud.

In that moment there was no right, no wrong—there was only Nick's touch and how it ignited desire in her. She pressed herself closer to him, needing to feel more of him against her.

Her hands sought his belt. She unclasped it and roughly whipped it off. He made a sound of approval deep in his chest and she continued to boldly, feverishly undress him. She didn't want anything between them. She'd waited too long for this. She didn't want to wait a second longer.

Once freed, his large shaft nudged against her hand and she grasped it eagerly. The size of it had her instantly quivering and wet. She wanted him, all of him, inside her. He groaned again as she stroked him, loving the length and width of him.

Straightening slightly, Nick laid his hands over hers. "Slow down. I want you to come first."

He lifted her and carried her to the counter, pushing aside what was there, sending a cake display crashing to the floor on the other side. "I'll replace that, too," he murmured against the sensitive skin of her stomach as he set her on the counter and sat on the stool before it. Rena balanced herself with her hands on the lip of the counter as Nick spread her legs wider. He ran the tip of his finger between her folds. "You're so wet for me." He slid one finger into her and rolled it.

Rena cried out in pleasure. "Oh, yes, that's it. Let yourself go, Rena. Let yourself enjoy this."

Rena leaned forward and kissed him with all the boldness he'd kissed her with earlier. She circled his tongue with hers, invaded his mouth with a hot abandon, like no kiss she'd given before. She sucked at his tongue, pulling him into her mouth, welcoming him, opening wider for him.

He caressed her breasts with one hand, gently rolling her nipple between his fingers while his other hand pumped in and out of her with growing speed. Rena was writhing against him when he broke off their kiss and trailed his mouth down her stomach to her wet center. He parted her lower lips and blew on her exposed clit.

Rena's hands clung to the counter.

He circled her nub with his tongue, flicking it with ever-increasing speed, until Rena couldn't think about anything except how much she wanted that tongue inside her. When he thrust it inside, she jutted against his mouth, calling out as wave after wave of release washed over her.

And still he didn't stop. He rubbed his thumb back and forth over her clit as he worshipped her inside and out with his tongue. He brought her from sated to crazy with need before he paused.

He stepped back and Rena felt that loss so intensely she called out to him, begging him not to stop. He was back a painfully long moment later. This time he stood between her legs, his hands finding her hips. He'd sheathed himself in a condom.

Her lips sought his even as his tip teased her swollen folds. With one powerful move, he lifted her, thrust himself inside, and claimed her mouth fully with his. She wrapped her legs around his waist and loved the ease with which he lifted her, adjusting her so he could drive himself deeper.

He went slowly at first, allowing her time to accept him fully. Then he withdrew, and drove himself inside her again. There was a wildness about their mating, and Rena gave herself to it completely. She met him thrust for thrust. She reveled in the feel of his tongue deep inside her mouth, dancing with hers in primal ownership.

He took her spiraling toward another orgasm and pounded into her as she came for a second time. Only then did he give himself his own release.

The only sound in the shop as they both came back to earth was their heavy breathing and the hum of traffic outside. He lowered her back onto the counter but didn't pull himself out. Instead, he kissed her lips gently, then held her there, still intimately entwined, and buried his face in her hair. "That was better than I've ever imagined—and I've spent a good deal of time imagining it."

Rena playfully tightened her inner muscles around him. "Me too."

His hands clenched on her thighs. "Why did we wait so long?"

Rena gasped when she felt him begin to stir and harden within her. "Because we both knew it was a bad idea."

He moved his hips, growing harder and larger as he spoke. "It doesn't feel so bad." He turned to the side and, having withdrawn, removed his condom and let it drop to the floor. The sound of him tearing open another foil package echoed through the otherwise silent shop. He pushed himself inside her again and leisurely stroked her from inside. "In fact, it feels so good I'm not done yet."

Running her hands over his chest and down his flat stomach, Rena tightened herself around him again—this time clenching and releasing with rhythm. "I don't want to talk anymore, Nick."

A pleased smile curled Nick's lips. "Me either."

He leaned over and scooped some of the fruit off a tart the owners had left for them. With a wicked grin, he smeared it on one of her breasts, then slowly licked it off, all the while gently thrusting his cock in and out of her with a slow and steady rhythm. "I'd hate for these to go to waste."

Rena buried her hands in his hair and threw her head back as excitement rocked through her. "Shut up and fuck me, Nick."

She felt him chuckle against her breast. "My pleasure."

No, Rena thought as his pace began to increase within her. *Mine.*

❧

"Did you bring a laptop to take notes, or would you like me to type up what we discussed today and email it to you?" Rena asked as she shimmied back into her dress. She then hunted for her shoes, struggling not to meet Nick's eyes. "It won't take much to get you up to speed on the project, but I think you should know how we've handled the unexpected in the past."

He smiled as he pulled on his slacks. "There will be time to talk about work later. Right now, all I want to do is teleport you back to my place so we can take a nap, then wake up and do this all over again."

Rena blushed and balanced on one leg as she slid a shoe on. "I can't go to your place, Nick."

"I don't mind your —"

She raised a hand. "And you can't come to mine. No one can see us together."

Surprised and more than a little offended, Nick said, "So I should cancel my order for the 'I fucked Rena' banner?"

That finally got her to look at him. She put her hands on her hips. "Joke all you want, Nick, but I'm serious."

Still bare-chested, Nick closed the distance between them and pulled her into his arms. He waited until she once again raised her eyes to his. "Are you worried about Gio? I'll talk to him."

"Don't. Please don't." Rena laid both her hands on his chest, and that alone was enough to send Nick's pulse racing. "This was great, but we both know it can't happen again."

"We do?" Nick frowned. He hadn't thought past how he'd intended to have her, but he didn't like the idea that what they'd shared was all he'd have of her.

She gave him a small smile. "Obviously we're attracted to each other. We're young, single, and human. Something like this was bound to happen eventually. But now we can put it behind us and go back to being friends."

"We've never been friends, Rena."

She inhaled quickly and smacked his chest. "That's an awful thing to say."

"You'd rather I lie?" She pulled back in his arms, but he held her there. He wasn't sure what he wanted, but he knew it didn't involve letting her go.

"Well, you might not care about me, but I have always cared about you..."

"I didn't say I didn't care about you."

"You just said—"

"That we've never been friends. I see that changing. I like being with you, Rena. I don't care what my brother thinks."

"You make it sound so simple, Nick, but it isn't. You know it's not." Rena raised a hand and caressed Nick's cheek. "You and Gio are finally getting along. I won't be the reason that changes. We can't repeat what we did today, and no one can ever know about it."

Nick frowned. "Let me get this straight. You fucked me because you care about me, and you're not going to fuck me again because you care about me."

She looked down at his chest and said weakly, "Yes, but I wouldn't put it as crudely."

"I have a different proposal."

"Proposal?" she looked up at him with rounded eyes.

"I say we do whatever the hell we want, and anyone who doesn't like it will have to simply get over it."

Rena closed her eyes and took a deep breath. "That's not going to work for me."

He ran a hand under her chin and tipped her head back. She opened her eyes warily. "What are you really worried about, Rena?" A sudden thought occurred to him. "My family or yours?"

"My family—"

"Has no right to tell us what we can or can't do."

"You can say that, Nick, but they would never allow me to hang out with you."

"Can you hear yourself? How long will you let them dictate how you live your life?"

"What would be better? Becoming like you? At least I'm close to my family."

Nick rested his chin on her forehead. "Ouch."

Rena wrapped her arms around his waist and laid her head on his chest. "I'm sorry. I shouldn't have said that. That was awful."

Nick sighed. "No, it was honest." He dropped his arms and stepped back from her. "Go get your laptop. I do need to be updated on the project."

Rena hesitated. "Nick, I..."

He grit his teeth. He was done talking about what Rena did or didn't want. The mere mention of his family was already souring his mood. "The notes, Rena. Get your fucking notes."

Chapter Eight

A WEEK LATER, Rena was dressed in yoga pants and a T-shirt, cleaning her house and swearing as she did. *Sure, I told Nick that I couldn't see him outside of work again. Yes, I reiterated that what we'd done was a one-time deal and absolutely could not be repeated. Okay, so my last parting words to him when I left the coffee shop were that it was best if we both tried to forget that anything had happened.*

But did he have to listen to me so completely?

Bastard.

Nick had been in and out of Rena's office all week as he'd confirmed the details for his meeting with Durkin and the congressman. Never once had he been anything less than professional. He'd come in the morning of the meeting to pick up some paperwork and had smiled briefly when she'd wished him luck.

Even the flowers he'd sent on Friday, a perfectly appropriate bouquet of white roses, had blandly said, "Thank you for all your help on the Durkin project."

Jackass.

It was supposed to be as hard for him to move on as it was proving for her. Every time she closed her eyes, she imagined him pulling her to him, his hot kisses on her neck, his cock thrusting inside her. Every time she saw him she wanted to run up to him and tell him she'd been a complete idiot. *Tell whoever you want, whatever you want—just don't smile at me like what we did didn't matter.*

Rena almost knocked over a lamp, then righted it at the last moment. *What is wrong with me? I don't agree with casual sex. Well, maybe for others, but not for me.*

She half closed her eyes and remembered what it was like to be lifted onto the counter of the coffee shop. She played back every touch, every sensation from that day with painful vividness. Nothing in her prior relationships had compared to what she'd experienced with Nick.

There had been nothing casual about that.

That was primal.

Consuming.

Heaven.

Rena shook her head. *And, apparently, completely forgettable for someone like Nick.*

Asshole.

Adding salt to her wound, Janet now regularly floated in and out of Rena's office. At first it was for advice. Then she'd dropped in to thank Rena for the advice. Now, she was beginning to stop by as if the two of them were friends.

"Want to go to lunch?"

"I'd rather staple my finger to my forehead," was what Rena wanted to say, but she made up excuses why she was busy instead. There was nothing outwardly dislikable about the young woman, but Rena feared she would stab her with a cafeteria fork if she said Nick's name one more time.

In the beginning, Janet had at least called him Mr. Andrade, but more and more she slipped and called him by his first name. "Nick would like a copy of this report... Nick wanted to make sure you received the geo map from the surveyors... Nick. Nick. Nick."

The doorbell to Rena's house rang and she jumped, this time sending the lamp crashing to the floor. She gave herself the luxury of a quick glance in the mirror, but what she saw didn't please her. Her eyes looked tired and her hair was tangled. *I'm a mess.*

She peered out the peephole on her door. A young man dressed in a delivery service uniform stood there with an envelope in his hands.

She opened the door. "Hello."

"Are you Ms. Sander?"

"Yes."

"This is for you."

"Who is it from?"

"He didn't say."

Rena took the envelope in her hand and weighed it thoughtfully. "Do you know what it is?"

"No, ma'am," the boy said and waited.

"Oh," Rena said. "Hang on." She returned with a tip, then closed the door when he'd left. There was no writing on the outside of the envelope.

She opened it.

It contained one box seat ticket to that night's performance of *Aida*. Rena thought of who might have invited her. She didn't remember anyone asking, plus why wouldn't they hold onto the ticket if she were going with them?

There wasn't even a note.

It didn't make any sense and felt more like a game than a gift.

Nick.

Rena shivered with a mix of excitement and apprehension. Was this his way of showing he was still interested in her? He wanted to take her out for a real date?

Was the opera his idea of a high-class, in-your-face announcement that they were together?

But we aren't—together, that is.

Even as she located her phone and readied it to text, she reminded herself of all the reasons why seeing Nick again would only cause trouble with both of their families. Gio would assume Nick was seeing her for nefarious reasons. Nick would risk losing Gio's trust. Kane and her parents would never approve. Kane would overreact—along with Gio.

There goes my job.

Am I ready for that?

Of course, the ticket might not even be from Nick and I could be worrying about nothing.

Rena texted her question: **Did you send me something via messenger?**

She held her breath and waited for his response.

Yes.

Since when do you like opera?

I don't. I find it boring.

So, why invite me?

Because you don't like it either. Which makes it perfect.

I love opera. I've been many times.

Your parents love it. You go to make them happy.

Nick's insight into what motivated Rena was unsettling. **I never said that.**

You never had to. I know you better than you think I do.

His text sent a confusing rush of pleasure through her. She didn't enjoy opera, but her parents loved taking her so she'd never said a word about it. *He does know me, even the parts of me I try to deny.*

His next text came before she had time to answer his last: **Come to *Aida* tonight. Wear the dress I'm having delivered to you.**

Nick, if we're seen together in public—

Do you trust me?

It wasn't an easy question to answer. She'd known him for most of her life. He was impulsive and often defiant in the face of authority, but he'd never involved her in anything he thought could hurt her. **I do trust you, but...**

Text me when you get there.

She wanted to say yes so much that not doing so brought a shine of tears to her eyes. His persistence forced her to face the largest hurdle between them: her fear. She grasped for a safer alternative: **I don't know, Nick. Maybe if we went somewhere more private.**

He didn't respond.

She added: **We shouldn't do this at all.**

No answer.

Finally, she typed, **I'm not going**, and dropped the phone into her bathrobe pocket. *Jerk.*

A few minutes later her doorbell rang again and another messenger delivered a large black-and-white box. Hugging the package in her arms, she spoke to her empty living room. "You are making it very hard for me to say no, Nick."

She laid the box on her couch and held its contents out in front of her. It was a strapless, floor-length shimmering blue gown with a slit cut high up one thigh. The material was light and designed to cling. It was definitely sexier than anything she would have chosen for herself.

Her phone beeped with an incoming message: **Do you like it?**

She typed back: **It's not my style.**

Try it on.

It's too small.

Tell me how you look in it.

Rena shook her head, then relented. She could argue it out with him, but part of her wanted to see how it would look on her. She stepped out of her clothing and slid the dress over her head. It fit her perfectly but left very little, if anything, to the imagination. She'd worn plenty of gowns in her life, but never one like this. The thin material hugged her curves intimately, bordering on indecently. **I can't wear it in public. I'd feel...** She almost said naked, but stopped herself. **Ridiculous. It barely covers anything.**

Sounds perfect.

For someone you'd hire for the night, but not for me.

So prudish. I love that side of you. You will wear it for me. You know why? Because we both know you want to.

Rena looked in the mirror and bit her bottom lip. Her nipples puckered beneath the thin material. Her eyes looked wild with desire and her cheeks were flushed pink. Saying no made sense, but saying yes was what she craved.

What are we doing, Nick?

Seeing you all week without being able to touch you has been driving me out of my mind. You don't want anyone to know about us, and I can't stop thinking about you. I'll play by your rules, Rena, if you play by mine. No one needs to know about tonight. Go to the opera, Rena, and go commando.

Commando? As in, no panties? Is he crazy?
There is no way I would ever even consider doing that.
No way.

⚃

That night Rena exited a cab in front of Lincoln Center and clutched the front of the long coat she'd thrown on over her gown. She stood outside by the fountain and looked for Nick but didn't see him. After gathering her courage, she stepped into the grand lobby of the Metropolitan Opera House. She'd seen these chandeliers many times before, but that night they shone extra bright. All of her senses were heightened. The fall air felt crisper. The deep rich reds were lusher. The paintings on the walls looked more sexual than she'd ever noticed.

She sent Nick a quick text to announce that she had arrived, then searched the crowd. Some were acquaintances of hers, but many more were complete strangers, and she suddenly didn't want to hide anymore. She shrugged off her long coat and checked it.

She turned back toward the crowd and felt—free.

And beautiful.

She'd swept her hair up off her neck and had carefully applied just enough makeup to bring out her eyes and high cheekbones. Some of the men around her stopped paying attention to their dates and gave her blatantly appreciative looks. Rena held herself proudly and had to admit she'd never felt sexier than she did that night.

She could feel people watching her as she walked past them. Women glared at her. More than one made catty remarks as she walked past and Rena bit back a smile. Never in her life had she imagined she could enjoy that type of attention.

Naughty really could feel nice.

She walked up to her private box alone and was disappointed to discover it was empty. Six seats were placed in two rows. Behind them was a curtain, designed to block the light from the hallway should the door open during the performance. She sat in the back row, but was still visible from the box seats across and adjacent to her.

What did I think he would do—buy out the theatre like he'd bought out the coffee shop?

As she sat alone, waiting for the lights to dim, she began to feel a little ridiculous. She checked her phone for a message from Nick but there wasn't one. She was tempted to go back down to the lobby to look for him, but she forced herself to remain seated.

The door behind the curtain opened and Rena held her breath. An older gentleman in a tux unfolded a small tray and placed a bottle of champagne on it. "Your champagne, ma'am." He popped the cork silently and poured a glass. One glass.

If Nick were joining her, wouldn't he have requested two glasses? She accepted her drink graciously but felt confused. Maybe he'd changed his mind? *Maybe we're only meeting afterward?* If so, it'd be a long wait. The opera was nearly four hours long.

After the waiter left, Rena sipped her champagne and resigned herself to once again pretend to be interested in *Aida.* Yes, the singing would be beautiful. Yes, translations were now projected onto a screen so a person could know what the singers were saying. But Rena had been born missing the gene that allowed people to enjoy prolonged bouts of dramatic singing.

The lights dimmed and a hush fell over the audience. In the quiet of the first act Rena heard the door behind her open. The woman in the box next to hers frowned at her, and Rena smiled back apologetically. Had Nick sent up sandwiches to go with the champagne? Shrimp cocktail, perhaps? Or was this when she'd receive the note explaining why he hadn't been able to make it?

"Rena," Nick's voice whispered from behind the curtain. "Come here."

Rena turned in her seat but all she could see was the plush velvet door curtain. "Nick?" she whispered.

The woman in the box beside her shushed her and Rena held in a giggle. She skirted out of her chair and pulled the edge of the curtain back to peer behind it. Instantly she was yanked behind it and gasped as she was pulled into the arms of a man she hoped was Nick. She couldn't tell because of the absolute darkness the curtain provided.

Nick placed a hand over her mouth and whispered in her ear, "If you want to keep us a secret, don't get us thrown out." He kissed one side of her neck and said, "I am going to take you right here, right now." He kissed his way across one of her exposed collarbones and murmured, "Even when you come— and you will come for me, Rena—don't make a sound."

With her heart beating crazily in her chest, Rena nodded. Nick removed his hand and kissed her. He dug his hands into her hair and plundered her mouth thoroughly until Rena was shaking with need against him. She clung to the cotton material of his dress shirt and gave herself over to the experience.

This was the passion her life had lacked.

He ran a hand down her back, over her ass, and along her thigh until he found the high slit in the dress. He shoved his hand beneath it and made a soft approving sound deep in his chest when his hand found no barrier to her already wet center. He dipped a finger inside her, then two, stroking her intimately while he continued to explore and ravage her mouth.

He leaned her back and spread her legs wider for his hand. His technique was one of confident expertise. He alternated rubbing her clit with thrusting his fingers in and out in a steady rhythm. Each time he reentered her, Rena clenched around his fingers and hot ecstasy shot through her. She fought to contain her moans, to keep her head enough to stop from crying out as wave after wave of pleasure rocked through her.

With his free hand, he lowered the bodice of her gown, exposing her breasts to his hungry mouth. He took a nipple roughly between his teeth, nipping at her in a way that had her throwing her head back and losing control. "Oh, yes," she gasped out.

Nick covered her mouth with his hand and chuckled. "Do I need to stop?"

She violently shook her head. *Oh, God, no.*

He rewarded her by moving his mouth to her other breast and nipping expertly at it as well. Rena shook and writhed against Nick, seeking more. She wanted to rip off her own dress and give his mouth full access to her. She wanted to cry out for him to plunge into her right then. No more waiting.

He increased the tempo of his magical fingers, and Rena bit her lip to stop herself from sobbing as a wild orgasm overtook her. He kissed her as the spasms rocked her body and she finally sagged against him.

He removed his hands from her, and she would have fallen to his feet in a satisfied puddle if she hadn't been holding onto his shoulders. She heard him undo his belt and zipper. Although she couldn't see it, she felt the tip of his rock-hard shaft against her stomach when he freed it. He sheathed it in a condom, then lifted her against the hidden side wall of the opera box.

Rena pulled his mouth back to hers and shivered with anticipation as he raised her gown and adjusted her to accept him. The emotion and volume of the singers rose, mirroring the passion of their kisses and the frenzy of their touch. She opened herself to him, wrapping her legs around his waist. He thrust deeply into her and withdrew, thrusting again with more force. She met his movements with her own, loving how he filled her. Again and again, each time deeper and deeper, until Rena felt a second orgasm building within her.

As the song reached a crescendo, Rena gripped herself around him, came with a shudder, and absorbed the moan that accompanied his own release. He held her there, intimately pinned against the wall, while their breathing returned to normal. Slowly he withdrew, then lowered her to stand.

He adjusted his clothing while she pulled her dress back into place, and then she was back in his arms as he whispered, "I fucking love the opera."

She laughed softly. "Me too."

He whispered, "Now you'll have something to think about when you come here with your family."

"I don't think I could ever come here with my parents again," Rena whispered back with another quiet laugh.

He licked her neck with his hot tongue. "You will, and when you do, you'll think of me inside you. I like that image. You sitting there all prim and proper, wishing I was there to fuck you. Getting wet and remembering how you came for me right here." He set her back from him and said, "Go back to your seat, Rena."

"We're staying?" Rena asked softly.

He didn't answer, and Rena couldn't see if he nodded or not. She took a step out from behind the curtain only to hear the door behind it open and shut.

Nick was gone.

Rena was half tempted to chase after him, but that wasn't part of their deal. She retook her seat and smoothed her dress down over her legs. The woman in the next area glared at her. Rena raised her hand to her hair and realized it was now hanging loose around her shoulders.

Rena smiled shamelessly at the disgruntled older woman. *Glare at me all you want, those passionate secret lovers down there would completely understand what I just did.*

Nick had forever changed how Rena saw the opera. Suddenly the songs held more meaning, and the emotion, which formerly had seemed overdramatic, was now poignant. She understood the fear, the uncertainty, and the pleasure that could be found in giving in to a lust that could not be contained.

She stayed until the end, and for the first time cried at the sheer beauty of it.

❦

After leaving the opera, Nick bypassed the bar and the VIP section of Skal. He found Serge in the club's office and plopped onto the couch just inside the door. He knew he had a huge silly grin on his face but didn't care.

Sex with Rena was better than any alcohol buzz. More addictive than any illegal substance. It made him feel— invincible.

"Well, you look pleased with yourself," Serge said and left his desk to sit in a chair beside him. "Does that expression on your face come with a story?"

"No," Nick said unapologetically. He propped his feet up on the coffee table in front of the him.

"Does she have a name?"

Nick shrugged. "Does it have to be about a woman?"

"No man looks that dopey happy for any other reason."

Dopey happy. Well, that was as good a description as any. "Touché, but that's all I'll say. I actually care about this one."

Serge propped his own feet up. "So you came here because you're happy about something you can't talk about?"

"Yes." Nick's smile widened.

"Is she married?"

"No."

"Underage?"

"Hell no."

"Actually a man, but you didn't realize it until it was too late?" Nick laughed out loud, and Serge threw up his hands. "It happens more than you'd think," he said, lightheartedly defending his suggestion. "But, hey, love is love. I don't judge."

"She's not a man." Nick relaxed deeper into the couch. "She's more than I expected, that's all."

"Tell me you're not talking about that sweet woman who came to see you here. That one I warned you to stay away from?"

Nick shrugged.

Serge slapped a hand on one of his thighs. "I knew you wouldn't listen to me."

Nick raised one eyebrow at Serge's uncharacteristic display of emotion. "You've never cared who I've dated."

Serge continued, "I'm trying to save you from making a mistake you'll spend the rest of your life regretting. It never works out with men like us and women like that."

Nick surged out of his seat. "I'm not doing this tonight. I *was* in a great mood."

With a sad expression on his face, Serge stood slowly. "Wake up, Nick. You want the suburban dream—wife, house, kids—as much as a shark wants to bake on the beach. And that woman—"

"Rena."

"Is the kind who won't settle for less than a ring on her finger."

"You don't know her."

"I know women."

"Right. I've never seen you with the same one for more than a month."

"Because I know myself, too. I tried to change for a woman once and ended up nearly destroying both of our lives. You're heading down the same path."

"I'm not you, Serge, and Rena knows the score. We're having fun. No harm. No foul."

"Hardheaded. Just like me." Serge folded his arms on his chest and shook his head.

Nick sighed. Serge had been too good to him for too long for Nick to stay irritated with him. Unlike his family, Serge was uncomplicated. Nick didn't second-guess his motives. If Serge was getting involved it meant he really was concerned. "How has business been?"

"Good. How about you? I heard you're doing well at Cogent."

Nick rolled back on his heels before answering. "It's interesting. Gio is a powerhouse, and the company is ahead of the pack when it comes to finding new energy resources. I have a lot to learn, but it's a challenge I'm enjoying."

"So, you and your brother patched things up. That's good."

Nick grimaced. "Nothing has changed, but we have a truce for now. I've kept my visits with my mother brief. That helped immensely."

"That's what you came to talk about, isn't it?"

Burying his hands in his pockets, Nick nodded. His questions weren't about Rena—they were about how being with her affected everything else. "I thought I needed the truth to be happy, but maybe I don't. I started working at Cogent to find answers, but I didn't expect to enjoy being there. I look forward to going to work every day. Rena is part of the reason, but so is everything else about the job. Gio and I used to talk about running the company together one day. Do you think I'm nuts to believe that's possible?"

"Ah, you're asking the wrong man. I don't talk to my family. I haven't in twenty years."

Nick rubbed his chin roughly. *That was my old solution.* With the security granted by the substantial trust fund his grandparents had left him, he'd never needed his brother's approval. Walking away had always been easy. Too easy.

He was only now beginning to see what it had cost him.

Serge stood. "But you're right—you're not me, Nick. I don't claim to understand why you want to be with people who drive you crazy, but you do. Just remember that seeking the truth about family is like looking at your ass when you're over thirty. It always leaves you wishing you hadn't."

Nick covered both of his eyes with his hand and groaned. "That's a vivid image I didn't need."

Serge chuckled. Nick joined him in a tension-relieving laugh. After a moment, Serge said, "Seriously, Nick, you came here for my opinion, so I'll give it to you. End it now."

"Working at Cogent?"

"And seeing your lady friend. Both situations have the potential of blowing up in your face."

Nick had found his own answers merely by entertaining Serge's response.

"It's not that simple," Nick responded. "I can't walk away. No matter what the truth is. I see that now." Then he walked away from Serge, heading out of the club. "And I won't stay away from Rena."

That would be like trying not to breathe.

Chapter Nine

RENA SMILED AND buried a tomato beneath a leaf of lettuce with a swipe of her fork, absently playing with her food. Even though she was having dinner with Kane and her parents, her mind was far away.

Would Nick call her that day?

What was he planning next?

Being with Nick was about more than the sex. She felt younger, sexier. There was a spring in her step that hadn't been there for years, and keeping the reason for it a secret was killing her. She'd spent the morning smiling at strangers and boldly meeting the eyes of the owners of the coffee shop near her house. She could tell they knew what she and Nick had done on their premises. But rather than feeling embarrassed, Rena wanted to lean in and say, "You think that was shocking? You should see what we did at the opera."

What had Nick said? "I'll play by your rules if you play by mine."

Oh, Nick, I like the way you play.

I like it a lot.

Her mother was retelling a week's worth of charity-related stories. Her father was listening kindly, as if she hadn't told him each story twice already. Kane was also dutifully attentive.

And I can't wait to return to the city to see if there is a message waiting from Nick.

She playfully stabbed at the tomato. It sailed into the air and bounced off her mother's shoulder. She knew she should apologize, but she was too busy reliving the feel of Nick's hands, the heat of his lips on hers. Waiting to experience either again was sheer torture.

"Rena," her mother said in gentle reprimand. When she didn't instantly receive an apology, she studied her daughter more closely. "Would you like to talk about whatever is on your mind before I wear your entire salad?"

"What?" Rena said, still somewhat bemused by her thoughts as she laid her fork down beside her plate. "Oh, sorry. I guess I'm distracted today."

"Out late last night?" her father asked, but his question held no bite. She'd never been a wild one so her parents didn't worry.

"I went to the opera," Rena said, a wide grin spreading across her face.

"I didn't realize you liked it," Kane said casually.

Rena bit her bottom lip. "I do now."

Kane's eyes narrowed at something in her expression.

Her mother leaned toward her and exclaimed, "You're glowing. You met someone, didn't you? What's his name?"

Rena blushed. Her father sat back in his chair and beamed a smile at his wife. "I believe you're right, Helen. But we shouldn't pressure her. We kept our relationship a secret in the beginning and look how we turned out. Rena has impeccable taste. I'm sure we'll love whomever she's seeing."

Helen took one of Rena's hands in hers and said, "Just tell me, am I right? Are you seeing someone new?"

"Yes," Rena admitted. At her mother's exclamation of glee, Rena rushed to add, "But it's not serious. We've only gone out a couple of times. I don't want to say anything yet."

Only Kane look displeased. "Is he someone we know?"

"Weren't you listening, Kane? I don't want to talk about him yet."

Kane sat back, folded his arms across his chest, and said, "Will I want to wring his neck when I find out who he is?"

Helen laughed. "Thom," she said, addressing her husband, "tell Kane to stop teasing his sister. Rena is old enough to date whoever she wants and to tell her brother to stuff it if he doesn't like it."

Rena's father joined in the laughter. "Do you remember what Kane and Gio did to the first boy she brought home? How old were you, Rena?"

"Fourteen," Rena said and rolled her eyes at the memory. "And they hung him over the porch railing by his ankles until he cried."

Kane shrugged. "We wouldn't have if he had taken our warning to be good to you seriously. He shouldn't have smirked at us."

Rena defended the young man whose name she had long since forgotten. Her mood was taking a spirally downward quickly. "He was probably nervous. The two of you were twice his size. Do you know how hard it was for me to get a date after that? No one wanted to come here."

"If you're waiting for me to feel badly about it, you're out of luck. I'd do it again in a heartbeat if you brought him back." Kane held her eyes and said, "I won't apologize for protecting my sister."

"I didn't need your protection then, and I don't want it now." Rena pushed her plate back from her. "Can we talk about something else?"

Kane didn't look happy about it, but he let the topic drop. Helen asked, "So, how is it at Cogent now that Nick is working there? That must have been a surprise for everyone."

Kane growled. "Gio is making a huge mistake giving Nick the kind of access he has, but you know Gio—he sees what he wants to when it comes to Nick."

Thom nodded sympathetically. "It's best not to get involved, Kane. Let them figure this out on their own."

"Figure what out? Nick is doing an excellent job," Rena said, unable to stop herself.

"Of course he is," Kane answered sarcastically. "Gio is spoon-feeding him success, hoping it'll change him, but it won't. Nick is there to start trouble. I hope Gio realizes that before Nick causes real damage."

Rena tossed her napkin on the table and stood up. "I just lost my appetite. Excuse me."

Kane pushed his chair back and also stood. "Where are you going, Rena?"

Their mother walked over and put a hand on Kane's shoulder. "Let's have a nice meal. Calm down, Kane. Rena, are you okay?"

Kane frowned at his mother. "I won't calm down. Not while she's making a huge mistake."

"What are you talking about, Kane?" Helen asked softly.

"Don't say it, Kane. Even if you disapprove, it's my decision. Not yours," Rena said angrily. "And I may not have been able to stop you when I was fourteen, but if you so much as lay a finger on the man I'm seeing, this will be the last Sunday dinner I share with you. I'm serious. Back off, Kane. This is important to me."

Rena turned on her heel and walked away from the table. Behind her she heard her mother say, "Let her go, Kane. I'll talk to her."

Rena walked out of the dining room. She paused in the hall. Her emotions were all over the place. She was still feeling euphoric from the night before, but she was also furious with her brother. She regretted walking away from her parents, whom she knew would be worried.

I should have said nothing.

She retrieved her coat from the closet and slipped it on just before her mother joined her.

Helen said, "I could use a walk in the garden. Join me." They exited the house together and walked side by side through the English garden's stone path in silence. When they reached the center of the garden, just where a fountain stood, Rena's mother said, "You and Kane never fight. What's wrong?"

"Nothing." Rena kicked the small rocks she'd once used as wishing.

"Is it about the boy you're dating?"

"He's a man, Mom, and that's part of it. I'm just tired of Kane thinking he knows what's best for me. I'm not a child anymore."

"He loves you, Rena."

"I know, but that doesn't give him the right to judge me or tell me what to do."

"Feel like making a wish?" her mother asked, holding out a small rock to Rena.

"I stopped believing in those years ago."

"That's a shame, because there is something magical that happens when you toss a rock in the fountain. Maybe it works because it forces a person to voice what they really want. I don't know."

Rena looked up with skepticism, not believing for a second that her very practical mother relied on wishes for anything she wanted.

"You know your father and I started with nothing."

"I know, Mom."

"I wished for all of this—a loving husband and enough money so our children would have easier lives than we did. Now, I followed that up with hard work, but it all started with knowing what I wanted." Her mother studied her closely as she asked, "You have everything, Rena, why aren't you happy?"

Rena felt a wave of shame at her mother's observation. "I am," she said quietly, but corrected herself when she heard the lack of conviction in her own answer. "I thought I was." She buried her hands in her coat pockets. "Did you ever wake up one day and wonder who you would have been if you'd been braver? If you hadn't always said no because you didn't want to disappoint anyone? I used to think I worked at Cogent because I wanted to be there, but did I pick that job? Or did you and Dad say it was a good, safe place for me to start, and I went along with it because I wanted you to be happy? I used to want to do so many things that I thought you'd disapprove of. I wanted take vacations with my friends, study abroad, do some wild and spontaneous things just for the fun of it. But I never did, Mom. I think I said no too many times, and I lost myself somehow. "

Her mother picked up a stone and threw it into the fountain. "My mother used to say, each generation messes up their children simply by trying to do the opposite of what their parents did. Your father and I were raised with nothing, so we wanted you to have everything. We worried it would spoil you, so we were strict. We didn't want you to be soft. We wanted you to know right from wrong. We felt it was important for you to understand the value of hard work as well as the responsibility that comes with having more than others."

Rena picked up a handful of stones, letting them drop one at a time back to the ground.

Her mother sat on the edge of the fountain. "You've never broken our rules, Rena, but sometimes I wish you had."

Rena jerked her head up to look at her mother. "What?"

"Talk to me. What do you want that you think we wouldn't support? Who could you possibly be dating that you're afraid we won't accept?"

Rena sat next to her mother on the lip of the fountain. "Nick Andrade."

"Oh." Her mother repeated herself in surprise. "Oh."

"Don't say it, Mom. I really don't want to hear all the reasons that dating him is a bad idea. I don't care about them. I only care about how I feel when I'm with him."

After a long moment, Helen said, "I can see why dating Nick would be exciting. He's a classic bad boy. Charming. Handsome. Untamable. Those are all sexy qualities in a fantasy man. But in reality, he's an angry rich kid who refuses to grow up. You'd never be happy with someone like that, and you'd never be able to change him. No matter how hard you tried." A sad, nostalgic expression entered her eyes.

Rena's mouth fell open.

"Did you think your father was the only man I've ever been with? He wasn't. There was one man, a long time ago, who made me glow the way you do when you talk about Nick. But it wasn't real, Rena. Nothing that feels that good ever is."

"I thought Dad was the love of your life. That's what you've always told us."

"Don't confuse lust with love. They are two very different things. And don't give your heart to a man like Nick. He'll only break it." She took Rena's hand in hers. "Your father is a good man and I do love him. I made the right choice."

"Does Dad know about the other man?"

"No. But he helped me put my life back together after my heart had been broken, and forgave me when I lashed out at him for things that weren't his fault. I fell in love with his kindness and his patience. I didn't have to tell him someone had hurt me. He's a smart man. But some details are better left unsaid."

"You don't know Nick like I do, Mom. He would never hurt me."

Helen nodded, then picked up a small stone and tossed it in the water.

"What did you wish for?" Rena asked as she picked up a stone.

Her mother forced a smile and stood. "I'll tell you when you have children of your own. Come on, let's go back inside."

Before joining her, Rena said, "Please don't say anything to Kane or Dad."

"I won't." She looked at the rock still in her daughter's hand. "You look like you want to make a wish, Rena."

Looking down at the stone, Rena shrugged. "Maybe. I don't know what I want anymore."

"Then hold onto it until you do." Hugging her daughter, Helen said, "And know that I'm here for you no matter what you decide to do."

Rena wiped away a quick tear. "Even if you don't agree with my decision?"

"I won't even let Kane hang him from the railing."

Rena laughed at that. "You wouldn't have let him do it back then if you'd been home."

"Just like I won't let you get away with telling him you would cut him out of your life. Neither of you are perfect. You were right to set boundaries with him, but now you need to go give him a hug and tell him you love him."

"Mom—"

"Rena, don't argue. Just do it."

Rena laid her head on her mother's shoulder and said, "Have I ever told you how amazing you are, Mom?"

Laying her cheek on her daughter's head, Helen answered, "Not so amazing, hon. Just a mother who loves her daughter very much." She kissed her hair, then straightened her coat and said nonchalantly, "And you don't have to worry about Kane going after Nick. I'll kill him myself if he hurts you."

Before Rena left her parents' house that night, she slipped back out to the fountain and dropped in her rock, sending ripples through the water. "I want to be brave enough to be myself—whoever that is."

◌

Nick's conversation with Serge had kept him up for most of Saturday night. Did Rena think their time together meant more than it did? Was she romanticizing it into a relationship?

He didn't usually worry, but this was Rena. He cared about her. Yes, the sex between them was fucking fantastic. Seeing her again was all he'd thought about since he'd left her at the opera. But if she believed the sex was leading toward a ring and a future—she was setting herself up for a disappointment.

Can I live with that?

His cell phone rang. He checked caller ID and groaned before answering, "Hello, Mother."

"I haven't seen you in a week."

"I've been busy."

"Too busy to come see me? Luckily I have staff who check in on me between my doctor visits. I'll leave instructions for them to update you if my health takes a downward turn, since it appears you won't be around to see for yourself."

"You were looking much better the last time I saw you. You're fine, Mother."

"So now you're a doctor? Fantastic. I'll call mine and tell him I no longer need testing since my son can diagnose me over the phone."

Nick sighed. "Was there a reason for your call?"

Patrice made a small sound of disapproval, then said, "Yes. Madison told me you're working at Cogent now with George. Why am I hearing news about my own sons from someone like her?" No matter how many times Gio has requested his mother call him by the name he'd chosen for himself, Patrice continued to refer to her oldest son as George.

"Like her? Maddy is family."

His mother made another unladylike sound of disagreement in her throat. "Well, I'm glad someone told me what you were up to. Are you sure it's wise to work there again? Have you forgotten about the first time?"

"It's different this time, Mother. We're working together on projects."

"Oh, Nick, you can be such a fool sometimes. He's letting you think you're important so he can manipulate you. Winning is all he's ever cared about. Tell me, did you threaten him when you went to see him? I know you, Nick. You stood up to him and that scared him."

"I'm hanging up now, Mother."

"It doesn't matter if you believe me, Nick. You'll find out for yourself. George is afraid. I tried to protect him, but as I face my own mortality, I have come to peace with letting go of what I can't change. One day, the truth will come out about what he did, and I hope you're smart enough to protect yourself, Nick. He'll let you take the blame if he can. That might even be why he's allowing you to work with him now. Watch your back, son. Whatever George is telling you, he has his own interests at heart. He always has."

Nick hung up on his mother and dropped down on his couch. He hadn't asked her what she thought Gio had done, and he wasn't going to.

His family was choking on its own lies. Even Luke, the family's ever-optimistic moral compass, could not find his way through this maze of dishonesty. Even if he could find the truth, how much would it matter if it was wielded as a weapon? Who do you trust when every story has multiple versions?

Eventually—no one. Was his mother right? Was Gio lulling Nick into complacency by throwing token projects at him? Could he be hiding something?

Or was Gio right? Was their mother's poor health fictitious? If so, why? And what would she gain by keeping Nick from working with Gio?

What is left to believe in when you can't trust the people you should the most?

Chapter Ten

TO CALL OR not to call.

After leaving her parents' house, Rena weighed that decision the entire ride home. With any other man, the answer would have been simple: Hell no. She didn't chase men; they chased her. Good-looking, hardworking men asked her out often enough that she'd never had to. Much of that, she knew, was due to her family's financial status.

Not an ego-boosting realization.

During the first few dates, it was nearly impossible to know if a man was genuinely attracted to her or just hoping to be the son-in-law of Sander Enterprises' founder. By the third date she could usually peg the social climbers. Spending more time at dinner talking to her father than to her was one certain giveaway. But there were others, worse offenders, whom she tried to forget.

One man had actually given her what looked like a business proposal for their one-month anniversary. He'd listed all of the reasons why merging their two families would be lucrative for everyone involved—even including a projection for increased profit margin after they announced their engagement.

Rena had pretended to read over the list carefully, running her finger down the long column to the end, then had said, "Quite a comprehensive argument, but it doesn't include the one reason why I can't marry you. I could never fuck a calculator."

Seeing the agitated expression on his face had been almost as enjoyable as crumpling his proposal and throwing it back at him. But Rena wasn't known for having a temper. Those who had known her since childhood often described her as a warm, supportive friend. Sweet. Predictable.

Boring.

Not at all who I am when I'm with Nick.

She thought of all the times she hadn't gone for what she wanted because she'd been concerned about how others would feel. She'd gone to a local college so her parents wouldn't worry. She'd taken a job her parents approved of because she knew they wanted her to be safe. Looking back, she'd even dated only men she thought her family would approve of.

She thought back to the wish she'd made in the fountain. *I don't want to live like that anymore. I'm done with tedious first dates and boring kisses that leave me wondering what is wrong with me. Doesn't everyone deserve some passion in their life? A reason to get out of bed?*

Just this once I don't want to be sensible. I don't need anyone's advice.

I want to be the woman I am when I'm with Nick.

Her mother might be right. He might one day break her heart. But she was willing to accept that possibility over never feeling the heat of Nick's kisses again.

Rena pulled her car into her garage and applied the brakes with more force than usual. She stepped out of the car and decisively slammed the door behind her.

I don't know what tomorrow will bring, but I'm doing this.
For me.

She flew up the steps to her house, barely touching them in her excitement. Once inside, she found her laptop, plopped down on her couch, and searched for a place she could take Nick.

Somewhere as private as a closed coffee shop, yet offering the thrill of getting it on at the opera. Somewhere that would impress even someone as experienced as Nick.

After searching for only a few minutes, she came across something that fit perfectly with what she was looking for. She called the place to confirm her plan was possible, then sent a text to Nick.

Come out to play with me next Saturday.

She held her breath and waited for his response.

Not tonight?

Not tonight.

I want to see you—now.

Don't say yes. You can have what you want if you do this right. Mom got hurt because she thought the man she was with would change for her. I know Nick. He won't change for anyone. He's so afraid of commitment he stays in a hotel instead of leasing an apartment. Only a fool would fall in love with a man like that.

And I'm no fool.

We can do this. We just have to do it in a way that ensures neither of us gets hurt. We'll contain it—control it. **You said you'd play by my rules if I played by yours. Well, here are mine. We keep this a secret, and we only meet on Saturdays. I'll plan this coming weekend; you can plan the next.**

And on the other days?

We're both free to do whatever we want. We'll see each other because we both work at Cogent, but during the week we're just friends.

Saturday sex. I like that.

Me too, Rena thought, running the tip of her tongue across her bottom lip. So far sex had been on his terms, but her arrangement changed the dynamics. They'd be partners of sorts—in a game of pleasure. **I already know where I'm taking you this Saturday.**

To your bed?

Nothing that boring. That's another rule. We don't come here, and we don't go to your place. This isn't a relationship. No one sleeps over.

Sounds like you know exactly what I want.

I hope so. **Yes.**

Then I'll see you at work. Goodnight, Rena.

Goodnight.

Rena dropped her phone beside her, closed her eyes, and smiled. *Oh, my God, I did it.*

C3

Early Monday morning, Nick walked through his secretary's office without stopping to greet her. Not going upstairs to see if Rena was at her desk was torture. Never before had a few days loomed so heavily between him and what he wanted.

And he wanted Rena—badly.

Any guilt he'd felt about seeing her was gone now that he knew she wasn't looking for a relationship. For her, he would have tried to be a boyfriend. He would have ridden out the wrath of his family and hers if she'd wanted him to. But that wouldn't be necessary, because he and Rena wanted the same thing.

Sex—pure, untainted-by-complication fucking.

He sat down at his desk, amused by how even the thought of being with Rena gave him a hard-on, and absently shifted through the notes Janet had left for him. He turned on his computer, checked his emails, and caught himself smiling in the reflection of his monitor.

Janet knocked on his door. "Nick?" When he didn't answer, she said, "Mr. Andrade?"

He shook his head and looked up. "What do you need, Janet?"

"Did you see my note about Mr. Westlake? He called late Friday afternoon."

"Mr. who?"

"Tad Westlake. He said you know him. His father owns Westlake Developments."

"Oh, Mad Tad. I haven't heard from him in months. You should see him when he drinks tequila. Give him a beer and he's as mellow as jello. A few shots of tequila, and someone's getting bailed out of jail. I hope I wasn't his one phone call."

Janet's eyes rounded. "He did sound upset."

Nick leaned forward and riffled through the notes on his desk. "If it was important, why the hell am I hearing about this now?"

Janet's hands fluttered nervously around her as she hastily defended herself. "I didn't know if I should bother you on the weekend. I'm not used to actually being a secretary. I hope I didn't screw anything up for you. I'm so sorry."

Nick took out his phone and raised one hand. "Relax. It's probably nothing. I'll call him now."

Janet nodded and started to leave.

Nick called out, "Janet."

She looked over her shoulder at him.

He winked at her and said, "You're a better secretary than I am a boss. We'll get there."

"Thanks, Nick," Janet said with a smile and closed the door behind her.

After she had gone, Nick compared the number he had on his phone to the number Tad had left. It was the same. Well, he wasn't in jail. How serious could it be?

"Nick, it's about time," his old friend said in place of a greeting. "I've been trying to reach you all weekend. I was beginning to think you weren't taking my calls anymore."

Nick leaned back in his chair and swiveled to look out the window. "Why would I do that?"

"I thought you were pissed at me." Tad lowered his voice. "Listen, you disappeared a few months ago. People said you went into rehab. Some of us heard you were dead. I didn't know what to think."

"Oh, so that's why you called all those times to see how I was. Wait, you didn't call. Not once."

"See, you're pissed. That's exactly why I thought you might be dodging me."

Nick rubbed one of his temples in irritation. He was in way too good of a mood to deal with this. "Tad, I don't care that you didn't call. I don't care what you need from me now. I'm not angry, but I don't have time for this shit."

"Don't hang up. I'm in trouble, Nick, and it's your fault."

Despite how things had gone recently, Nick couldn't leave Tad hanging if he really was in trouble. Especially if it was somehow Nick's fault. He swung his chair back toward his desk. "What happened?"

"My dad found out you were working for your family's company and he's been all over me about it. He won't let up. He says if someone like you can grow up and become responsible, then so can I. Now I have this huge fucking office and I have to wear a goddamn suit every day."

"Oh, poor Tad. That really sucks." Nick didn't try to hide his sarcasm.

"You don't even know how badly it does. He told me that if I don't land a new contract, any contract, he's going to cut me off."

"That's your father's favorite threat. He never follows through."

Lowering his voice even further, Tad said, "He took my driver and fired my cook. I'm driving a rental car, for God's sake. I called for the jet last weekend and the pilot told me no. Didn't even ask me why I needed it. Just told me to contact my father with future requests. He's serious this time."

"Then it sounds like you should start making some phone calls."

"Don't jerk me around, Nick. That's why I called you. Cogent could use my father's company on one of its projects. You know it could."

"Which project?"

"Any fucking project. I don't fucking know or care. Just help me, Nick. You've got to help me."

"Hold on." Nick skimmed his emails for a correspondence he'd had with someone about a possible site in Guinea. The country's government was looking for a developer to come in and mine bauxite. It was a small contract, and one that didn't project a large profit margin for Cogent, unless they could find a developer who would do it cheaply. "I could probably subcontract you for a job in Guinea, but you'd have to make a really low bid. I mean, ridiculously low."

"It's my dad's money, I don't care. And it might be enough to get him off my back. He won't cut me off for making a bad choice as long as I bring in something."

"I'll send some paperwork over by tomorrow."

"Thanks, Nick."

"Sure. What are friends for?" Nick said icily and hung up. He gagged at the thought that he and Tad had once had enough in common to hang out. It made him take a new look at who he had been, and he didn't like what he saw.

"You didn't come to see me this morning," Gio said from the door of Nick's office.

Nick stood as he remembered that he'd set a meeting with his brother. "Sorry, Gio. I don't know where my head is today."

"That's okay," Gio said calmly, taking a seat in front of Nick's desk. "You're here, and it looks like you're working, so that's good."

"I may have just gotten Westlake Developments to low-bid us for Guinea," Nick said, "which would make that project a go for us."

"No shit," Gio said, clearly impressed. "How did you land Westlake? I've been trying to crack them for years. They don't budge on their profit cut."

"I know the son, and he was looking for a deal. I offered it to him and he was desperate enough to take it."

"A friend of yours?"

"Not really. Not anymore."

Gio nodded again, slowly. "Business and friendships are a tough mix. Many people say family and business are worse, but you've proven you belong here, Nick. I'm proud of you."

In that moment, Nick once again felt the urge to seek answers to questions that had plagued him. "Gio, you said Cogent had been in financial distress when you took it over. I looked back at what you did when you started here. How did you find the capital for the projects you took on?"

Gio met his eyes and said, "I emptied my trust fund to back them."

Nick swallowed hard. "So if Cogent folds, you're bankrupt?"

"Yes."

"No wonder you fight so hard for it."

Shaking his head, Gio said, "I fight so hard for it because it's our legacy, Nick. Our family built this. Our great-grandfather purchased the land this building sits on. That matters to me. Doesn't it matter to you?"

Nick inhaled sharply. "It didn't use to." He studied his brother. "How far would you go to protect that legacy?"

"As far as I had to."

There it was, the dark side of his family. Dark enough to make Nick think his brother might be capable of whatever their mother thought he'd done. It made him remember what Serge had said about digging for the truth about your family. It never ends well.

"And to protect yourself?"

"What are you asking, Nick?"

I need to know, even if it's ugly. "Mother implied that you had done something you were afraid I'd uncover. Something that could ruin you. She warned me you might try to pin it on me."

Gio's jaw tightened and a red flush spread up his cheeks. "Our mother is a piece of work, isn't she?"

"You didn't answer the question. Are you hiding something, Gio?"

Gio stood and shook his head with disgust. "I would never let you take the fall for something I had done. Never. If you don't believe anything else, believe that." With that, Gio walked out of Nick's office.

Which means he is hiding something. Nick punched the side of his desk with such force that Janet came running in.

"Is everything okay, Nick?"

Nick rubbed his swollen knuckles. "As okay as it's ever been." When Janet continued to stand there looking concerned, he said, "It's fine, Janet. Close the door on your way out."

He didn't know who he believed anymore, but he did know what he wanted.

Saturday sex with Rena.

He leaned back in his chair and closed his eyes.

It was going to be a long week.

Chapter Eleven

A FEW DAYS later, Rena was seated at her desk, typing up a memo. She paused, looked at the door, and cursed. She was finding it impossible to concentrate. Nick and Gio were out of the office for a meeting with Westlake Developers. It was the first time Rena had seen them together for a client meeting. It was a new contract that Nick had landed. The fact that Gio had told her anything about it proved it was an important one.

She had seen Nick once since hearing about Westlake. They'd met by accident in the hallway the day before. Rena had smiled at him politely, reminding herself of her own rules.

Nick, dressed in a Corneliani suit and looking as comfortable as if he'd always worked at Cogent, had given her a roguish smile that implied he was tempted to say more but was willing to play along. "How are you, Rena?"

"Good," she'd answered thickly, clutching her notebook to her chest.

"Did you have a nice weekend?" he'd asked in an innocuous tone that nevertheless sent a wild blush to Rena's cheeks.

"Wonderful." She'd inwardly groaned at her inability to form a coherent sentence when his chocolate eyes held hers.

"Do anything special?" His eyes had danced with both laughter and a heat that sent waves of fire through her.

Her embarrassment had faded as she'd realized he wasn't laughing at her but rather with her. She'd never had a secret, and sharing one with Nick was surprisingly fun. "I went to the opera."

"How was it?"

Rena had traced her top teeth lightly with the tip of her tongue, experimenting with this newfound connection. Nick's nose had flared slightly and his eyes had narrowed, giving Rena even more confidence. "Surprisingly good."

"The best you've been to?"

"Hard to say." Rena had hidden a saucy grin, trying to keep the conversation unremarkable to those walking past. "Each one is so different."

Nick frowned. His displeasure with her comment was so clear she wanted to tell him she was joking, but she didn't. Way too many women had contributed to his large ego; it wouldn't hurt him one bit to think he had to step up his game to impress her. "Planning anything interesting for this coming weekend?"

"I am, actually," Rena said, thoroughly enjoying their banter now.

"Anything you'd like to share?"

"No."

An entirely new expression crossed Nick's face, but Rena wasn't sure how to interpret it. She couldn't tell if he was irritated or turned on by their conversation. She changed the subject, saying, "I heard you landed Westlake. Cogent has been trying to work with them for years. How did you land that?"

Nick didn't hesitate. "Via the son. It's not a done deal yet. We meet later in the week to nail it down."

Rena remembered one of the reports she'd organized for Gio regarding rumors of Westlake's expansion plans. "I have a file you might want to look over just in case Daddy decides to play hardball. It was information Gio thought would be helpful last spring, but we ended up not needing it."

"And you're going to give it to me?"

"Yes. You want to do well here, and this will be good for the company."

"Why do you trust me?"

It was such a simple and heartfelt question, Rena had almost tossed her rules to the side and thrown herself in his arms. Instead, she clutched her notepad tighter to her and said, "Because I know you."

Nick had nodded once. "Send me the file."

Rena had taken a step back but added, "I will. Hopefully you won't need it."

Nick had leaned in and growled, "Waiting for Saturday is killing me."

Rena had winked at him as she turned away. "Good."

Nick had groaned behind her and Rena had floated all the way back to her office.

I hope I know what I'm doing, Rena thought as she turned back to her computer and reread the memo she should have finished an hour ago.

"Is this a bad time?" Maddy asked as she breezed into the office.

Rena considered saying it was, but it wasn't Maddy's fault her morning had been unproductive so far. "Gio's not here today."

Maddy picked up a photo on Rena's desk and studied it. "Who is the hunk with you in this photo?"

"That's my brother, Kane."

"That's Kane? Why did I not know he was gorgeous?"

"Because you're married?"

Maddy studied the photo carefully. "Not for me, silly. I'm cataloguing him in my head for future reference. Every chef needs to know what ingredients he has in his kitchen, if you know what I mean."

Rena stood and shook her head. "Not really."

"People think matchmaking is easy, but it doesn't just happen. It takes time and planning. Is your brother single?"

"Yes, but he's not looking for anyone right now. He's married to his company."

"If I had a nickel for every time I heard that one."

Rena took the photo back and replaced it on her desk. "You didn't come here to discuss my brother."

Maddy shrugged. "You're right. I was hoping to shamelessly pump you for information about Nick and his secretary. He hasn't fired her yet. How close is he to falling for her?"

Rena sat back down at her desk. "I really wouldn't know."

"Have you ever been in love?"

Rena knocked over a cup full of paper clips, made a wild grab for them, then swore when they scattered across the rug behind her. "No."

"Then you may not know what to look for. Is he distracted lately? Do you catch him smiling at odd times? Watch for changes in his behavior. That's usually a sure sign."

"I told you—I'm not getting involved in this."

"Sure, you said that, but now you've had time to think it over. Janet is perfect for Nick. She's sweet. She's honest. From everything I hear, they get along really well. I just want confirmation of the rumors."

Rena slapped a hand down on her desk. "How many times do I have to tell you no? No, I'm not helping you hook Nick up with his secretary. I'm not watching the two of them together to see how they get along. Do you know why? Because I don't care how close they are or aren't. It doesn't matter to me. Now can I get back to work?"

"Oh, my God, you like him."

Rena froze. "I don't."

"Oh, my God, you're the woman from the photo at the bar. I didn't see the resemblance until just now."

"I'm not."

"You should have told me. Of course you don't want to fix Nick up with his secretary. You want him for yourself." Maddy leaned forward across her desk. "I feel awful for not guessing sooner. You must hate me."

"I don't."

"You poor thing. Does he know? Of course he knows, because you were kissing him in the photo."

"That was a joke. Nothing more."

Maddy clapped her hands together. "I could teach a detective course. See, I wasn't even sure it was you but I thought I'd take a chance. Amazing how that works, isn't it? It's because I have a sense about people. That's why I'm so good at matching them up."

Do you also know when they want you to leave their office?
Rena kept that thought to herself.

"Come out to lunch with me. I have to rethink this whole plan. You and Nick. This changes everything."

"There is no me and Nick."

"Maddy, I could hear you all the way down the hall," a deep male voice said from behind them.

Maddy turned and threw her arms around Luke, crushing him in a hug. "Luke, why are you here today?"

He hugged her warmly, then replied, "Gio called and said he and Nick have a reason to celebrate. I had a window of time open so I thought I'd meet them for lunch. What trouble are you starting now?"

Maddy's eyes rounded. "It's a secret."

Luke looked across at Rena sympathetically. "Then you two probably shouldn't be shouting down the hallway."

Rena lunged from her chair. "Did anyone else hear us?"

Luke shook his head. "Not that I saw. So what is this about you and Nick?"

"There is no me and Nick."

Maddy let out an audible sigh. "She likes him."

Rena spun on Maddy and snapped, "You are the world's worst secret keeper."

Maddy threw up both hands in triumph. "I knew it."

Luke walked over and looked down at Rena. "Is there something going on I should know about?"

"No," Rena and Maddy said in unison.

Rena glared at Maddy, who shamelessly smiled back at her. Scrambling for damage control, Rena said, "Maddy doesn't understand that I've known Nick my whole life. Of course I like him. He's like a brother to me."

Maddy raised an eyebrow. "Oh, you can lie with a straight face. I'll have to remember that."

Luke looked back and forth between the two women. "Rena, I hope you don't have feelings for Nick. He and Gio are finally getting along."

"I know," Rena said and rubbed her forehead roughly. "I would never do anything to endanger that."

"Why can't Rena and Nick get together?" Maddy asked.

Luke held Rena's eyes. "Because if Gio found out, he'd never trust Nick again."

"Which is why," Rena said slowly, "nothing will ever happen between us."

Maddy took one of Rena's hands in hers. "I had no idea. This is so sad. Luke, couldn't you talk to Gio? Get him to soften his opinion about it?"

Luke didn't look away from Rena. "I wouldn't even try. I don't think they belong together either."

Maddy cocked her head to one side and studied Luke's expression. "Do you have feelings for Rena?"

He shook his head. "Not the kind you're referring to, but I do care about her. Too much to ever let her date my brother. He's coming around, Rena, but he's not the one for you. Your heart goes out to him because you know what he's going through, but he needs to figure it out on his own. If this goes badly, I don't want him to pull you down with him."

"You could improve his chances of succeeding here, Luke, if you showed a little more faith in him." Rena folded her arms across her chest as she voiced the one opinion she was comfortable sharing in this conversation.

The tension in the room was as thick as the silence that dragged on was long.

"Awkward," Maddy said with some humor as the standoff continued.

Rena didn't back down. "You could also try having a little faith in me."

Luke held her eyes for another moment, then sighed and said, "Sorry. This is the closest to happy I've seen my family be in a long time, and I don't want anything to ruin it."

"You don't have to worry because nothing is going on," Rena said firmly. She turned and pinned Maddy down with a glare. "Nothing. Are we clear?"

Maddy reluctantly agreed. "Gotcha. Nothing." She tapped a finger on the corner of Rena's desk, her irrepressible smile returning. "So, lunch, Rena?"

Rena shook her head and chuckled at Maddy's persistence. "Not today. I really do have a lot of work to do." She looked down at the paper clips strewn around the area behind her desk. "I should get back to it."

Luke took out his phone. "That's Gio. He and Nick are downstairs in a car. See you ladies later." Just before he walked out the door, he stopped and said, "Rena, I'd ask you to come, but—"

Rena gave him a small smile. "I know."

"Maddy? What about you?"

She looked down at her Cartier watch. "I've been away from the babies long enough." She glanced at Rena, real sympathy in her eyes. "Besides, I got what I came here for."

"I'll walk you down."

Maddy and Luke left together and Rena laid her forehead on her desk.

I probably should have gone to lunch with Maddy. She'll never keep this to herself. Hoping she will is like hoping the sun won't come up tomorrow.

Rena had watched how doggedly Maddy had pursued Gio when she'd wanted him to attend her cousin's wedding. Hopefully this time she'd see that getting involved would only make things worse. Rena bent and gathered the scattered paper clips, returning them methodically to their container on her pristine desk.

Maddy didn't base her decisions on what others thought was best for her. As far as Rena had seen, Maddy made her own rules and expected others to love her for it.

Eventually everyone did. *So why do I think the world will come to a halt if I am caught doing what I want for a change?* She half smiled as she thought about the coming weekend. *Or who I want?*

I can't let the possibility that Maddy might spill the beans ruin this for me.

Rena held the container of paper clips in one hand and studied them with a frown. *Maddy would never settle for boring. I don't want to anymore, either. And to everyone who thinks that I'll get my heart broken?*

You don't know me.

Heartbreaking is going to bed each night alone or, worse, with someone who makes you wish you were.

Rena tipped the container upside over the waste bin and emptied it. *I deserve fucking colorful paper clips. And amazing, mind-blowing sex on Saturdays.*

And I refuse to feel badly about that.

∽

During lunch at Sardi's, Nick looked across the table at his youngest brother, Max. "I had no idea you were in town."

"I'm looking into redeveloping an area in Secaucus." Max shrugged.

"In Secaucus?" Gio asked, mulling over the idea.

Max nodded.

"Have you purchased the property yet? I may have some useful connections," Gio offered.

Raising one hand, Max dismissed the idea. "Thanks, but you know I like to work things out on my own."

Luke reached for his glass. "Is it a casino?"

"No, it would be an expansion of my hotel chain. I haven't fully committed to the endeavor yet."

The reason wasn't a mystery to Nick. "He doesn't know if he can handle being that close to us."

Max groaned. "I went to see Mom. She's as crazy as ever. I couldn't get out of there fast enough."

"How did she look?" Gio asked casually, but he was watching Max closely.

"So, that part was true? You're not speaking to her?" Gio started to say something, but Max cut him off. "Forget I said that. I really don't want to know. I came here because Luke said we have something to celebrate."

Luke leaned in toward Nick. "I called him after I spoke to Gio about your meeting this morning. I thought he'd like to know that things are going well. I had no idea he was in town, but when I found out, it seemed like a perfect time for all of us to get together."

Nick looked quickly at Gio. "What did you tell Luke?"

Gio shrugged one shoulder. "Just the truth. Westlake was trying to play hardball and you backed him right into a corner— exactly how I would have done it. It was impressive. Luke usually hears about how I want to strangle you. I thought it would be nice to share something good for a change."

Luke added, "And I thought that sounded like something we should all celebrate."

Nick couldn't keep the sarcasm from his voice when he turned to Max and said, "So, essentially we're celebrating that I'm not a complete loser in the eyes of my brothers."

Max clapped Nick on the back and said, "We all hoped this day would come. Should we toast with beer? Champagne?"

Without missing a beat, Nick said, "I actually don't drink anymore."

That seemed to surprise Max, who looked at his two other brothers and asked, "Am I the only one here who is shocked to hear those words?"

Gio laid his napkin on his lap and picked up his menu. "I guessed as much when Nick showed up to work every day."

Luke smiled and followed suit with his own napkin. "People tell me everything. It's the price I pay for being the sane brother."

Max laughed. "Hey, I'm the sane one."

Nick picked up his own menu and spoke as if to himself. "Funny, I thought it was me."

In a much more relaxed manner than usual, Gio added, "I always knew it wasn't me. I got the looks and brains instead."

All three brothers jokingly made sounds of outrage. Max turned to Luke. "Nick is sober. Gio has a sense of humor. Are you a veterinarian now? Did I accidentally enter a parallel universe because I don't recognize any of you?"

The waiter came by, interrupting the conversation. After all four had given their orders and were alone once again, Nick said, "It was time I made a change. Something clicked inside me when I heard our uncles talking about family and how our father would have been proud of us. I didn't think he would be. Proud of me, that is. I hadn't done anything to make him proud. I wanted to be more like the rest of the Andrades and"—he looked around the table before continuing—"no offense, less like us."

Gio cleared his throat. "I felt the same way. So much of what I was angry about didn't matter anymore when I thought about the next generation. I don't want to be us, either."

Luke interjected, "We don't have to be. Yes, we have to be us, but we don't have to be at each other's throats all the time. We're not enemies, we're brothers."

Max studied each of his brother's faces. "You're all serious? This isn't some sort of sick prank? I'm sorry, I'm having a hard time swallowing this."

Nick smiled at his youngest brother. "Would it help if I told you that Gio is still an unbearably pompous ass most of the time? I just keep that fact to myself now."

Gio's eyes narrowed. "Or if I said that I'm waiting for the day human resources files a group complaint because every secretary in the building discovers she's not the only one he's sleeping with?"

"I haven't slept with every secretary. Aren't there hundreds? That would take me months."

A muscle in Gio's jaw clenched visibly. "Look me in the eye and tell me you're not doing something you shouldn't be and I'll relax."

Nick threw up his hands in the air. "You'd never believe me if I told you, so why waste my breath?"

Max started laughing. "Okay, I feel better. Now I know I'm sitting at the right table."

Luke said, "You can laugh, but they are much better than they were."

With a more serious expression, Max said, "I admire you, Luke, for always believing things will work out. I won't say I'd bet on you being right, but I admire your optimism."

Gio's hand clenched on the table. "When I was on Isola Santos I felt like an Andrade. And their motto is: Family is everything."

Nick shook his head with humor. "I wonder what the Stanfield family motto is?" He laughed sarcastically. "I'll have to ask Mother. That should be entertaining."

The meal arrived but no one moved to touch their food. Luke said, "It doesn't matter what the last generation of our family believed. We decide what our legacy will be. The four of us."

Gio nodded. "Speaking of the four of us, Julia and I are serious. We'll be picking a wedding date soon. I want the three of you there."

Luke said, "Of course we'll be there."

Max hedged. "It'll depend on my schedule."

With a frown, Luke countered, "You'll make time for your brother's wedding."

Unapologetically, Max shrugged. "Hey, I just did the big family wedding thing. I don't know if I can handle another of those soon. Tell me where you want to honeymoon, though, and I'll hook you up with a penthouse."

Nick shook his head. "Seriously, Max?"

With quick irritation, Max snapped, "Don't judge me, Nick. You've done whatever you've wanted, however you've wanted to, your whole life. Now, just because you're sober for a few months and working at the family company, you think you're the better brother?" He stood up and slammed his napkin down on the table beside his untouched plate of food. "I can't do this again. You had me fooled at the wedding. That's how this works. You lure me back with a promise of sanity and then the crazy returns. I'm happy you're all getting along right now. I don't believe for a second it's going to last, and I don't have the time or the energy to sit around and pretend I do. Send me an invitation, Gio, and if I'm free I'll be there." He turned to Luke. "Thank you for calling me today, Luke. I know you meant well."

Gio stood. "Sit down, Max."

Max looked at his oldest brother coldly. "You don't tell me what to do, Gio. You never could and you never will." With that he turned and walked out of the restaurant.

"He's beginning to sound like me," Nick drawled.

Gio sat back down, shaking his head. "I don't understand. He wasn't like that the last time I saw him."

Luke looked every bit as mystified. "He's not usually so angry."

"He must have stayed at Mother's five minutes too long," Gio said, then reached for his fork and knife.

Chapter Twelve

IT WAS TEN o'clock in the morning on a crisp fall day when Rena stepped out of a taxi and wiggled in an attempt to adjust her panties without touching them. She put her hands in the pockets of her blazer and tried to hold the elastics of her underwear while shimmying her ass back and forth. It didn't help, but she wasn't alone at the large flat field she'd driven to. *That's what I get for thinking I could do kinky well.*

After a few days of brainstorming how to make her day with Nick as sexy as he'd made their last romps, Rena had visited an adult toy store. She didn't consider herself a prude, but as she'd stared at the options displayed on the wall, all she could ask herself was, "What is that and who would use it?"

Thankfully, a woman had come over and asked if she could be of assistance.

"I'm looking for..." Rena had hesitated, blushed, then started again. "Something really sexy but not over the top."

"For yourself or for your partner?"

"For both of us?"

"Sure," the woman had said casually as if Rena had been asking to see a watch or bracelet. "Let me show you some suggestions."

Rena had taken one last look around the wall covered with enormous dildos, strings of beads, and plugs of all shapes and sizes and readily agreed, "Please do."

She'd followed the clerk to a section full of items she was comfortable with—basic vibrators. She'd received one as a joke at her housewarming party, and like the tool set she'd gotten, she'd eventually put it to use.

"I'll be taking it on a date," Rena said, without meeting the eyes of the other woman.

The clerk held up a box of vibrating thong panties and said, "These are very popular. You wear them and give your partner the remote control."

Rena accepted the package and her confidence grew. *I'm a grown woman, and there is nothing wrong with trying something new now and then.* She turned the package over and read the description on the back, then smiled. "It's perfect."

However, nowhere during the process of cashing out did the woman mention how intimately the underwear's mechanics would lodge itself if worn while driving. Or walking. Every time Rena moved, the bullet-shaped insert rubbed against her already excited clit and scrambled her thoughts.

And it's not even on yet.

This is going to be incredible.

A middle-aged gentleman dressed in a bright-yellow company T-shirt, his attire matching that of the other three men with him, waved her to approach. She did and hoped her gait didn't reveal her secret. "Good morning."

"Good morning, Ms. Sander. We have everything set for you." He shook her hand enthusiastically and introduced her to the other men on his team. "Is your friend on his way?"

"He should be," Rena answered, looking at the inflating hot air balloon and basket behind him. "How long will we be able to be up there for?"

"You paid a deposit and agreed to one hour, but you can have more time if you want it."

How long does one need to have a wild encounter in a hot air balloon? She studied the basket. It wasn't large enough to lie down in. *I guess we'll be standing up.* She bit her bottom lip. *That can be nice, too.* "How high will we go?"

I hope they won't be able to see us from down here.

"I can take you up twenty-five feet or a hundred, depending on the wind. So far everything looks like a go, but I like to make that decision when I'm up there."

When he's where?

Rena's head snapped around and she asked, "Don't you stay on the ground?"

Both of his eyebrows rose comically. "Ma'am, I'm the pilot."

Rena looked back at the balloon. "But this is a tethered ride. We just go up and then come down. We don't go anywhere. I'm sure we don't need a pilot."

"Did you read our website? We do tethered rides at fairs and large events. You booked a regular trip."

"No," Rena said slowly. "So you can't just let us go up and then bring us down?"

"Lady, this isn't a kite. A balloon in a ten-mile-an-hour gust of wind could drag a couple of trucks with ease. We didn't bring the equipment to tether it."

"Oh, I was hoping we could go up alone."

"That wouldn't have been possible either way. You'd have to know how use the burner and the valves properly."

"Would you give me a quick lesson if I paid you double?"

"You're not understanding what I'm saying. As soon as it leaves the ground, it's a registered flying aircraft that requires a licensed pilot."

"How about triple? In fact, name your price. If you're worried about me damaging your balloon, how much could it cost? I'll buy it. Just give me the basics of how to work the damn thing." *Okay, I sound desperate, but you would, too, if you were wearing vibrating underwear and thought you'd be alone up there having a hour of wild sex.*

"I have a team assembled here for a reason. It's more dangerous than it looks. There is no amount of money that would make me risk my pilot's license. You go up with me, or you go home and forfeit your deposit. Your choice, lady."

"Looks like her friend is here," one of the T-shirt-clad men said when a car parked beside hers.

"You think he's as bat-shit crazy as she is?" another of them asked.

Rena spun on him and glared. "I can hear you."

He shrugged and tipped his baseball cap at her.

Rena stared longingly as Nick, dressed in jeans and a cable-knit sweater, stepped out of the back of a town car, a picnic basket in hand. Their eyes met and heat flooded through Rena. Everything around them faded away while he ever so slowly walked toward her. The grin he gave her was the sexiest thing she'd ever seen and knocked the air right out of her.

"I think I know why she wanted you to stay down on the ground, Hank," one of the younger men joked.

Rena kept a smile on her face and said, "I will tip each of you a thousand dollars if you don't embarrass me."

The pilot, stood beside her and said, "Best behavior, boys. With that kind of tip we could buy a new basket for the third balloon." He turned to Rena. "Besides, I'm guessing she wants a short flight now."

Rena nodded curtly. *This doesn't have to ruin our day. Nick doesn't know what I had planned. Be cool, Rena. Play this off like you planned it this way.*

℈

Nick walked across the grassy field to where Rena and a group of men were standing in front of a hot air balloon. He was surprised by her choice of location. He hadn't known what to expect when a driver picked him up at his hotel and handed him a picnic basket and a small wrapped gift, with instructions not to open either. Of course he'd opened both. The champagne and chocolate-covered strawberries had led him to believe she'd planned something more intimate than the option laid out before him now.

As for the remote control that he'd tucked into his jacket pocket—well, he hoped he was right about what that was for. He was tempted to find out right then and there, but decided against finding out in front of an audience.

The crowd didn't stop him, however, from walking straight up to her, dropping the basket, hauling her into his arms, and claiming her mouth with his. No, he'd waited all week to touch her again and nothing was going to stop him.

She met his kiss eagerly, opening her mouth to his. Her hands came up to rest on his chest and he shuddered from the pleasure of it. Nothing in his vast experience had prepared him for the desire that rocked him at her touch. He wanted to tell her to forget whatever she'd planned and haul her off to the nearest hotel. Hell, the nearest semi-private clump of bushes would soon do if she kept kissing him the way she was.

He cursed the layers of clothing separating them, damned the men standing nearby, and reluctantly broke off the kiss. Their ragged breathing mixed when he rested his forehead on hers. "I missed you."

She smiled. "You saw me every day."

He moved his head to speak softly into her ear. "Not like this."

"This is nice," she agreed with a sigh.

A man beside them cleared his throat loudly. "I'm Hank, your pilot. Are we ready to go?"

Nick didn't move, continuing to hold Rena tightly against him. "I know I am."

A concerned look darkened Rena's eyes. "Do you want to ditch the balloon ride? It seemed like a good idea, but I didn't think it through very well."

Had it been anyone else, he would have given in to the need raging within him and agreed, but as he looked down into her eyes, he realized that he wanted her to be happy more than he wanted anything for himself. It was a new feeling and one that scared him a little. He shook his head, dismissed that thought, and said, "It was a great idea. I've never been in one. Let's do it."

Her eyes rounded with surprise. "You've never been in a hot air balloon?"

He looked down at her, "Contrary to what you believe, I haven't done everything."

A spicy little smile pursed her lips. "Me either."

Nick inwardly chastised his throbbing cock for robbing him of the ability to think straight. *Down, boy, you'll have your chance later.* He stepped back from her, handed the picnic basket to the pilot, along with a substantial tip, and said, "Make it a quick trip."

"Absolutely, sir," Hank answered and smiled.

Nick and Rena followed him into the basket. Rena stood, holding onto the side of it. Nick moved to stand behind her and pulled her back against him. Shoving the picnic basket away from his feet, he felt for the remote in his jacket pocket. Knowing he could use it at any time brought a smile to his face as they lifted off the ground.

When the pilot brought the balloon to a nice cruising height, Nick and Rena could see patches of fields, trees, and homes below. Able to hear dogs barking below, their peaceful journey was interrupted only when Hank ignited the burner to raise the balloon higher.

"What an amazing view," Rena said, taking in the serene landscape.

"Not near as amazing as the one I have right here." Nick leaned in and nuzzled her neck from behind. Rena gasped as he pushed his legs between hers. "Am I right in thinking you're wearing something special for me?"

"I didn't realize we would have company. And it's too quiet to use it right now. It was a crazy idea anyway."

Right then the pilot gave the burner another push, shattering the silence. At the same time, Nick pressed the remote, giving Rena a quick jolt, which produced a louder gasp from her. Keeping his head close to her ear, he whispered, "Crazy is my middle name. We can make it work if you trust me." He reached one arm around her waist and caressed her, moving his hand up to cup and gently squeeze her breast. Rena leaned back against him, squirming as the remote sent vibrations through her.

With his back to the pilot, Nick continued to press against Rena and the remote. He turned his head to Hank and said, "How high can you take us? Can the burner run long enough to climb a thousand feet?"

Hank gave him a bland look.

As the burner powered up, Nick turned the remote to a higher and higher setting. Rena clutched at the edge of the basket in front of her, fighting for control as the bullet continued vibrating. "Oh God... Nick, the view is breathtaking... Oh my God, can we go just a little higher?... Yes, that's perfect... Don't change anything."

"I wouldn't." Never before had someone else's pleasure meant more to him than his own. He bent down to gently stroke his lips across her neck. His left hand skimmed over her breast, lightly pinching her aroused nipple. He felt her tense and her breathing quicken. She trembled and gasped. Nick hugged Rena tighter, his cock firmly pressed against her lower back, knowing she was about to explode. He held her firmly through the spasms until her body relaxed and her breathing slowed. He turned off the remote, then smiled against her neck.

She turned, wrapped her arms around his neck, and kissed him with such passion he almost forgot they weren't alone. Her hands ran through the back of his hair, her body arched against him, rubbing back and forth against his throbbing cock. He broke off the kiss and gripped her hips to still her, fearing he would lose his load right there. "Easy, Rena. I'm only human."

She smiled up at him. "You make me feel—free. I never thought it could be this way."

He pulled her tight to him, tucking her beneath his chin and seeking to calm his raging libido. He couldn't label his own feelings as easily as she had. He wanted to land the balloon, carry her to the first secluded spot they could find, and finish what they had started. Then he wanted...

That was the part of his fantasy where his heart started pounding wildly and his throat constricted. The rest of the day should be easy enough to imagine. Sex, sex, followed by more sex, then parting ways until the following Saturday.

Uncomplicated pleasure with someone he genuinely liked.

"Come back to my place after this," Nick said, surprising himself with his invitation.

Rena shook her head. "I booked a room for the afternoon at a hotel near the takeoff site." She smoothed one of her hands across his chest. "At the time I didn't realize this was an untethered ride. I should have read the description on the website better."

He covered her hand with his. "It was perfect."

She leaned back to look up into his eyes. "You made our first two times so amazing, I wanted to wow you." She blushed and lowered her gaze to his chin. "Sorry this part of the day wasn't as exciting for you as it was for me."

He brushed his lips over hers gently and murmured into her ear, "It was perfect, but I can't wait to get you alone. I want to see your face when you come. I want to feel you tighten around my cock as you orgasm and cry out my name. And then I want to start all over, slowly, taking my time getting to know every inch of you. An afternoon doesn't sound like enough time for what I want to do."

"It'll have to be," Rena said with an expression he couldn't decipher.

Instead of answering her, Nick turned to the balloon pilot and said, "How soon can you land us?"

"There is a clearing just over those trees. I've landed there before. Easy access from the road. I'll radio down to my team." A moment later, Hank said, "Everything is set. Your driver is following my team so everyone should be there."

"Good," Nick said, then leaned down and whispered in Rena's ear. "If my time with you is limited, I don't want to waste another moment up here with him."

Desire flared in Rena's eyes. "I booked a suite with a heated indoor pool. I've never been skinny-dipping."

Nick nuzzled her neck. "If I have my way, you won't have energy left for a swim."

☙

Rena climbed into the back of Nick's town car feeling as if she were in some erotic dream—one she wouldn't wake from feeling frustrated. No, this particular dream just kept getting better and better.

Nick slid in beside her, and Rena was surprised when he left a chaste space between them. He leaned forward, instructed the driver to take a scenic route back, and told him to turn on the radio.

"Any particular station?" the driver asked.

"Doesn't matter," Nick said, glancing across the seat and holding Rena's eyes with his. He slid one hand into his coat pocket. "Just crank it up." The air sizzled with anticipation as the vehicle filled with the pulsating beat of Iggy Azalea.

The car pulled out of the field onto the road. When nothing more happened, Rena began to think she'd misunderstood Nick's intention. He half turned in his seat and looked at her.

Is he going to turn it on or not? Rena bit her lip. *What the hell is he waiting for?*

Silently, he mouthed, "Is this what you want?"

The vibration in her panties started, but at such a low setting it was nothing more than a tease. Rena flipped her chin upward in what she hoped was a universal sign for more.

His mouth curled with a devilish smile. "Like this?" he asked, his voice just barely audible above the music. The vibration intensified by the smallest of fractions.

Rena mouthed back, "More."

He put it on full speed. Rena gasped, gripped the door handle beside her, and closed her eyes. Nick lowered the speed back to a hum, and Rena's eyes flew once more back to his.

"Keep your eyes open," he ordered.

Helpless to deny him, Rena did and was rewarded by the bullet vibrating wildly against her clit. All the while, Nick watched her expression, clearly enjoying the game. As she became more excited, she squirmed in her seat to adjust the bullet so it could caress her with even more accuracy. Just when she thought she was going to orgasm, he lowered the speed.

Rena shook her head in protest.

Nick merely smiled and started to increase the speed again, slowly, then let it ebb away. What had at first been frustrating became its own sort of caress. Like the lapping of a tongue, the vibration came and went rhythmically. Each time it returned, Rena tightened as heat shot through her. Each time it ebbed, she wanted to cry out against the loss.

The orgasm building within her felt stronger each time it almost crested. Rena desperately reached out one hand toward Nick. He brought it to his mouth, running his tongue along the inside of her wrist. The sensation of his hot, wet mouth on her skin sent Rena over the edge. She gripped his hand tightly and fought to keep her eyes open while her orgasm rolled through her, wave after wave. She sagged against her side of the car.

He closed the distance between them and growled into her ear. "Next time you come you'll be on your knees with me in your mouth."

Rena shook with need at the image. Waiting was its own pleasure, and pain. She needed more than her damn toy. She wanted his hands on her. She wanted him inside her—yes, in her mouth and, God yes, in any other way he wanted to be. She was tempted to drop before him in the backseat of the car, despite their lack of privacy, and bring him to the place he'd already taken her to twice that day.

She wanted him as out of control as she felt. She shifted to do just that, but he pulled her to his side. "Not yet, Rena. Patience."

The rest of the ride was sheer torture. Just when Rena began to calm, he teased her with just enough vibration to rev her up again. And each time she thought he had changed his mind and would give her another release, he stopped.

By the time they reached the hotel, Rena was wild in a way she'd never imagined she could be. She waited in a daze beside Nick while he checked them in. As soon as the elevator door closed, she pulled his mouth hungrily down to hers and cried out, "Fuck yes," when the bullet once again began its dance against her.

This time, though, she could taste Nick, and she couldn't get enough of him. His tongue wrapped around hers, guiding her to a rhythm of his choosing. Her hands sought his hard shaft and rubbed it eagerly through the material of his slacks. The elevator opened and they stumbled together into the private hallway outside their hotel suite.

Without breaking the kiss, he inserted the key, and the door swung open behind them. Rena was beyond caring about where they were, her hands frantically unbuckling his belt. She made quick work of the front of his pants and fell to her knees before him, pulling his pants down to his ankles as she went.

His cock, hard and proud, sprung up before her, and she took it greedily into her mouth. One of her hands cupped his balls while her other clung to his muscular thigh. She felt the bullet go wild against her clit and took him even deeper into her mouth.

There against the open door of the hotel room, he leaned back, dug a hand into the back of her hair, and held her to him while he thrust deeper into her. She welcomed him as she'd never welcomed another. Desperately. Wantonly. His pleasure was her pleasure, and the added benefit of her own stimulation sent her into a frenzy.

He gave the back of her hair a forceful tug and she raised her eyes to meet his. "I'm going to come," he said as if giving her a chance to withdraw.

She opened her mouth even wider and lapped at the side of his cock. When she felt him tensing beneath her hands, she gave herself to her own orgasm and they came in near perfect unison.

He stepped out of his pants and shoes, pulled her to her feet and kicked the door shut behind them. She was still in a near speechless daze. He picked her up and carried her to the bedroom, tossing her down on the bed and slowly removing his jacket and shirt.

"Nick," she said, putting a hand up to stop him before he joined her on the bed.

His expression instantly became concerned. "What it is, Rena?"

She waved a hand in the direction of his clothing. "Turn off the vibrator."

He looked down at her and laughed without doing as she'd requested. "I forgot it was on." He slowly removed her shoes and her clothing until she was lying in front of him with only the silk panties on. He lay beside her and put his hand on top of the bullet, holding it even more firmly against her. "Are you sure you want it off?"

"It was good," Rena gasped, "but now it's too much."

He leaned down and kissed the curve of her breast, then moved to lick a circle around her nipple. "I believe the point of giving me the remote is that I get to decide how much is too much."

Beneath his touch, the vibrations leapt to a new level. Rena felt it rippling through her. Nick slid a finger inside a slit in the panties, and he kissed each of her breasts thoroughly.

There was no reprieve, only more and more sensation until Rena thought she had nothing left to give. His finger played gently in and out of her wet folds, and Rena began to writhe back and forth beside him. Nothing she'd ever experienced had come close to how she felt right then. He sheathed himself in a condom, positioned himself between her legs, and thrust deeply into her.

The object she would have considered a barrier between them instead acted as another point of connection and subtly changed how he felt inside her. He paused after each deep thrust, and the toy she had thought had already enjoyed thoroughly moved him within her.

"You are so wet, Rena. So tight. I should have licked your come off you like you licked mine off me. And I will."

He rolled onto his back, taking her along so she was straddling him. He lifted and lowered her slowly onto him, then held her in place while his tempo increased.

Rena held onto his shoulders and leaned down to kiss him passionately. Her final orgasm was a subtle flood of heat that started in her head and spread down through her toes. She was floating down to earth after it when she felt Nick reach his own climax. He shuddered and clutched at her, releasing his load in one final deep thrust.

Rena collapsed on top of him.

Nick removed her panties, tossed them onto the floor, disposed of his condom, then took her in his arms. Rena wondered if there was a medical term for how relaxed she felt. She vaguely felt Nick pull one of the bedsheets over them.

In the blissful aftermath, her eyes began to close, but one final thing stood in her way. She whispered, "The vibrator is still on. I can hear it."

Nick chuckled and kissed her shoulder. "The remote is in my coat pocket. I'd have to get up to turn it off."

Rena snuggled closer to him and gave a moan of protest. "I'd offer to do it, but I can't move."

Nick chuckled again. "No swimming?"

Rena shook her head and laughed tiredly. "Maybe after a nap."

Pulling her even closer, Nick murmured, "If I only get one day a week, I can think of better ways to spend our time than swimming."

Rena was so relaxed that she couldn't protest, and she wasn't sure she wanted to.

Skinning-dipping was probably overrated anyway.

Chapter Thirteen

"I'M SORRY, WHAT did you say?" Rena asked the young woman at the sub shop on the Cogent building's first floor.

The woman repeated herself in a rush. "Did you want the dressing on the side? I put it on the salad. I can make another but it will take a minute."

Rena smiled and held out her hand. "I'll take it. It's all good."

And it had been for nearly five weeks. Rena couldn't remember a time when she had been happier. She and Nick had fallen into a routine of speaking casually all week at work, then running off together somewhere amazing each Saturday.

Her cheeks warmed as she remembered some of the locations. By private jet, he'd flown her to Bermuda, where they'd made love in crystal caves illuminated by warm artificial lights. Nothing was off limits to a man with enough money. Although Rena wasn't as well off as he was, she was financially comfortable. Comfortable enough to fly him up to Niagara Falls, where she'd chartered a private boat on which they'd made love to the roar of the water crashing down around them. Great sex, exotic locations— more than that, Saturdays had become a day when Rena felt free to be herself.

She had joked that they were partners in crime, and Nick had responded that it was better than that—they were partners in pleasure. And pleasure was something her life was presently so full of, it spilled over into the weekdays that led up to her next rendezvous with Nick.

He seemed just as happy with their arrangement. Everyone mentioned how much he had changed since he'd started working at Cogent. They said he'd grown into the confident businessman Gio had always said he could be.

Rena liked to think she had something to do with that, although he didn't need her help now nearly as much as he had in the beginning. If she explained a process to him once, she could bet not only that he had understood it, but that he would come back with an improved version of it soon afterward. She felt as good about how they worked together as she did about how they played together.

"Ma'am? Ma'am?" the woman behind the counter pulled Rena back to the present.

"Yes?"

"You already paid. Did you need anything else?"

Rena realized she was standing at the register, salad in hand, a huge smile on her face, as a line of impatient customers grew behind her. "Oh, sorry. No, I have everything I need."

And more, Rena thought and sighed with satisfaction as she turned away from the counter.

"Rena."

Rena turned to find Julia, Gio's fiancée, standing close beside her.

"Are you on your lunch break?"

Shaking her head to clear it, Rena said, "Yes, for a few more minutes. How are you? I haven't seen you around much." Before she stepped out of line, Rena asked, "Are you getting something?"

Julia smiled at the grumbling crowd behind them. "No, I'm having lunch with Gio in a little bit." They walked together to a small corner table and sat down. "I'm working like crazy now that my designs are selling. After Claire Danes wore one of my pieces to the Emmys, I couldn't fill the orders fast enough."

Rena went to take a sip of water, then realized she hadn't opened her bottle of water yet. As she fumbled with it, she said, "That's so incredible. Can you believe how much your life has changed in such a short time?"

"It really has," Julia said in a happy rush. "Even my parents are happier. Not that Gio wouldn't help my family if they needed it, but Dad was relieved when he made enough money from the sale of his company that he could afford full-time care for my mother. Now he can keep her at home."

"How is she?" Rena asked, reaching across the table to lay her hand on her friend's. Julia was not only beautiful, she was the most giving woman Rena had ever met.

"She'll never be better—Alzheimer's can't reverse course—but she's getting the best medical care money can buy, and my dad can spend more time with her now. That's important to both of them. She's less afraid when he's with her. And Gio is amazing with her. He introduces himself to her every time he meets her and he does it in a way that makes her smile."

Rena squeezed Julia's hand. "If there is anything I can ever do."

Julia smiled and returned the squeeze. "I know. And I hope you know it's the same for me. I'm here for you. You can tell me anything. Even if it's something you think you can't tell anyone."

Rena withdrew her hand and asked, "Did Maddy say something to you?"

Julia looked away. "No."

"Look at me, Julia. Did she?"

Julia reluctantly met Rena's eyes. "I don't want to cause any trouble between the two of you. I just want you to know I support you in whatever you do—even if you're doing something you think is wrong. Not that I think it's wrong. Actually, I don't really know enough about what you're doing to know if it's right or wrong, but—oh, hell, are you dating Nick?"

"Yes," Rena said, then added, "and no."

Julia rolled her eyes and leaned forward. "Well, that's as clear as mud. Are you or aren't you?"

Rena ducked in toward Julia. "You have to promise you won't say a word to Maddy. Telling her is like taking out an ad in a newspaper. I'm not saying anything unless you swear it'll stay between the two of us."

"You can trust me," Julia said with confidence.

Once Rena started talking about Nick, she couldn't stop. She told Julia about how long she'd known Nick and his brothers, and how important it was that nothing ruined the bond he and Gio were building by working together. She explained how she'd always had something of a crush on him, and how shocked she'd been the first time he'd kissed her. It wasn't until she started to explain their arrangement that Julia broke her silence.

"Wait, so you only see him on Saturdays?"

"Well, I see him at work all week, but we make sure we act like nothing is going on."

"What about Sundays?"

"No, never."

"Is that your choice or his?"

"It was my idea. He agreed to it."

"I don't get it."

"You asked me if I was dating Nick and I'm trying to explain it to you. Dating is two people building toward a relationship. We're not doing that. We're like friends... but..."

"With benefits?" Julia asked, her eyebrows rising.

"Yes," Rena said. "Corny, but accurate, I guess. Friends with benefits. Friends with very secret, no-one-can-know-about-them benefits."

"And you're okay with that?"

Rena smiled. "Oh, my God, it's incredible. I've never been better."

"Oh," Julia said as if she were still mulling over the idea. "If you're happy and Nick is happy, then I guess it's a good thing."

"A very good thing," Rena said. "But no one can know about us. Gio wouldn't understand, and my brother would lose his mind if he found out."

Julia pursed her lips in thought. "Normally I would say I could bring Gio around to the idea, but he has a lot on his mind this week. That was the other thing I wanted to ask you. Is something going on at Cogent I should know about? Gio's not himself and he won't tell me why. He says it's business related and leaves it at that. Did something happen?"

"Not that I know of." Rena sat up straight in her chair. "I have been distracted, though. You don't think he knows about Nick and me, do you?"

"No, he would have told me that. I guess I was hoping you'd heard something else. Nick hasn't said anything?"

"No. Nothing." Suddenly, Rena remembered something. "Gio did get upset with me on Friday when I couldn't tell him who had delivered a certain envelope. He was furious. I haven't seen him that angry in a long time. I offered to look into it, but he told me he'd handle it himself. Then I just forgot about it. Now that you mention it, he's been in a bad mood all week. I should have asked him more about it but I didn't. Sorry."

Julia looked down at her hands, then back up. "I don't understand why it's so hard for Gio to tell me what's bothering him. I could help him."

"Have you met his mother?"

With a visible shudder, Julia answered, "Yes. Okay, I guess I do understand. But what do I do?"

Rena gave Julia's arm a supportive pat. "I'll talk to Nick. Maybe he knows something."

"Would he tell you if he did?"

Rena thought about it, then with confidence said, "Yes, he would."

Later that day, while Gio was out for an extended lunch with Julia, Rena dropped by Nick's office. His drop-dead gorgeous secretary asked her to wait a moment while she checked if Nick could see her. Rena wanted to tell her what she could do with her ridiculously long nails and overly bleached hair, then lectured herself that it didn't matter what Nick's secretary looked like because she and Nick didn't have a commitment. That was part of the arrangement. No questions allowed about what either of them did when they weren't together.

Not that Rena was interested in anyone besides Nick.

And she didn't think he was seeing anyone else.

Certainly not this bimbo.

Before Rena had time to chastise herself for a moment of weakness, Nick was standing before her with that sexy, I'd-do-you-right-here smile on his face. "I love it when *you* come to *me*," he said, turning the simple declaration into an innuendo, wiggling his eyebrows for effect.

Janet rushed back to her desk.

Rena gave him a playful swat on the arm. She wanted to be upset with him for being less than subtle, but she also wanted to throw her arms around his neck and kiss him senseless for not caring what his secretary thought. "Stop," she said with a smile. "That's not why I'm here."

He took her hand in his. "It could be." His smile was all invitation as he whispered in her ear, "Have you seen the size of my... desk?"

Rena shook her head, torn between being drawn into his sexual banter and remaining businesslike. She forced herself to focus on the reason she'd sought him out. "I spoke to Julia today. She's worried about Gio. Can we talk?"

Instantly serious, Nick guided her into his office. "Absolutely." He closed the door behind them. "What's going on?"

Rena told him what Julia had said and then shared how Gio had responded to the envelope he'd received the week before. "Julia said Gio hasn't been himself this week. He told her it was work related. I don't know of anything that is going wrong at work. Do you?"

"No," Nick said, but he didn't look surprised.

He knows something.

Why did I think he would tell me if he knew?

We're just friends.

Barely that on Sunday through Friday. She fought back against the insecurities that nipped at her. *And I'm okay with it.*

I have to be okay with it.

"Well, if you hear anything, please tell me. Gio has been in a bad mood all week, so Julia might be right. There could be something wrong."

Nick shrugged. "Gio has been in a bad mood for years."

"Not since he met Julia. Not like this."

Nick pulled Rena into his arms and tipped her face up to his. "Hey, you're really worried about this, aren't you?"

"I am," Rena said, fighting the desire to wrap her arms around his waist and bury her face in his chest. She extracted herself from his embrace. If she gave into the pleasure of being with him even a little, she feared she would lose the tight control she'd maintained over her feelings. And she couldn't risk that.

"Rena," Nick reached for her again but she evaded him. "What's wrong?"

"Nothing," she said quickly. "We're at work, Nick. I don't want to... I can't..." She gave up trying to be strong and, in a moment of panic, turned and fled. She cursed herself the whole way back to her office.

Don't do it.

Don't ruin the best thing you've ever had because you can't follow your own rules.

ભ

Following Rena's abrupt departure, it didn't take Nick more than a moment to decide it was time to tell Gio he was seeing her. In the beginning, Rena's rules had been fun. The secrecy had made their time together even more exciting. But lately, Nick was becoming less able to contain what he felt for Rena to Saturdays.

He had started to call her during the week, but she'd asked him to stop.

He'd offered to drive her home from a dinner party they'd attended separately, but she'd refused. He was beginning to see that the very rules that had brought them together were now keeping them apart.

Although their escapades were fun, they weren't enough for him. He wanted Rena in his bed on more than just one day, and he was prepared to do anything to achieve that goal.

If he'd thought being around her would make him want her less, he couldn't have been more wrong. She'd become an obsession to him.

He sent Gio a text to come see him when he returned to the office. It was time to remove every obstacle standing between him and Rena.

As he rehearsed how he'd tell Gio, he remembered what Rena had asked him. If something was bothering Gio, it would be better to ask him before rather than after his announcement in case it was something urgent.

Nick didn't doubt for a moment that Gio would storm off in a huff as soon as Nick told him he'd been seeing Rena, but he was confident they were now close enough that he'd get over it.

Rena would be the harder one to win over.

Why she clung to her rules so adamantly was beyond him, but he was sure if he planned their makeup sex just right, not only would she forgive him, she'd also be in his bed whenever he wanted—which would be every night.

Chapter Fourteen

RENA WAS BACK at her desk sorting Gio's mail when her cell phone rang. She hesitated before digging it out of her bag. If it was Nick, she wasn't ready to talk to him yet. If it was Maddy, she definitely didn't want to talk to her. Kane? Not now. Mom and Dad? Please no. Really, the list of who she was in the mood to speak then was near nonexistent.

Still, her phone continued to ring, so she gave in and answered it. "Hello."

"Rena, I hope I haven't caught you at a bad time."

Almost dropping the phone, she was so surprised by the voice that greeted her, Rena strove to sound casual as she said, "Patrice. I didn't realize you had my number."

"Of course I do, dear, you're practically part of my family."

Her tone set the hairs on the back of Rena's neck standing on end. Like a snake trying to hypnotize its prey, Nick's mother was always nicest before she struck. "How are you feeling?" Rena asked, attempting to be polite. Patrice could have won an Oscar for the performance she dove into. She made a small, pathetic sound as if she were in pain, then claimed to be feeling better. Rena rolled her eyes heavenward and prayed for strength.

"Are you with George?"

"No, he's still at lunch."

"So, you're alone?"

"Yes."

"I'm worried about Nick. He and George have never gotten along well. It must be difficult for him, trying so hard to fit in where he knows he'll never be welcome."

"It's not like that, Patrice."

"Really? How is it?"

Don't trust her. Don't say anything. "They're getting along really well. I've never seen Nick happier."

"And you would know what makes Nick happy, wouldn't you, Rena? I hear you've been spending time with him lately."

Maddy wouldn't have said something to Patrice, would she? "We do work at the same company, so yes, that's true."

Patrice laughed, but the sound held more malice than humor. "Don't lie to me, dear. I know what you're up to, but I won't tell anyone—as long as I can count on you to help me."

As much as Rena wanted to hang up on Patrice, she needed to know what the old bat was after. "What do you want, Patrice?"

"What you want—the best for Nick. He'll never be happy as long as he lives in George's shadow. Help me convince him to quit Cogent. He doesn't need a job. He has more money than he could ever spend in his trust fund."

Rena let out a harsh breath. "Patrice, your sons are finally getting along. You should be happy."

"Don't tell me how I should or shouldn't feel. If you care at all about Nick, you'll help me."

"It's because I care about him that I won't."

"You think you know everything, don't you? I've had to stomach watching you insert yourself into my family for too long. I was hoping to avoid this, but you've left me with no other choice. You can either convince Nick to quit Cogent, or you can watch me destroy him."

Rena gasped at the ugliness in Patrice's voice. "What are you talking about?"

"I know my boys better than anyone else. I know exactly what it would take to get him drinking again, and then he'll help himself right out of his new job. Push me and I'll show you the real Nick."

"You don't mean that, Patrice."

"No? You don't want to be on my bad side, Rena. I can turn all of them against you, and I'll start by showing the world what a little whore you are. Do you think you and Nick weren't seen?

Weren't photographed? The tabloids love a good scandal. Could you say the same about your parents?"

As disgust rose in her throat, Rena's temper soared. "I don't know what happened to you or why you're as bitter as you are, but I guess I should have expected this phone call. I heard about how you threatened Julia. You scared her, but you don't scare me. And you don't have the control over your sons that you think you do. Not anymore. They are so much more than who you see when you look at them. And they love you, even though you don't deserve it. You want to hurt me? Bring it on. Try to turn them against me. You'll lose. And then, maybe, you'll finally see how loyal and loving your sons really are."

Rena waited for Patrice to counter with her own threat.

She readied herself for whatever form it would take.

Patrice said nothing for a moment, then there was a sound as if she and the phone had dropped to the floor.

Does she really think I'm going to fall for this?

"Patrice? Patrice?"

She didn't answer. Rena heard ragged breathing and a faint moan in the background.

It'll be a cold day in hell before I call 911 for her.

"Patrice. You can stop pretending. You're not fooling anyone."

Rena hung up her phone, then started pacing back and forth. *No one believes Patrice had a heart attack. This is just another attempt on her part to use the sympathy card.*

Rena tried to call Patrice back, but there was no answer.

Dammit.

She almost called Nick, but she thought about what Patrice had said about driving him back to drink. Was this part of her plan to do that?

She called Luke instead. "Luke, I think your mother just had another episode. She was on the phone with me. Should I call nine-one-one?"

He asked her for the details of exactly what had happened then, said he'd send an ambulance over and meet it there. He hung up without another word and Rena sank into the chair behind her desk.

Gio and Julia walked in, arm in arm, laughing over something. They took one look at Rena and froze. "What happened?" Gio demanded.

"Your mother may have collapsed. Luke is on his way to check on her. I was on the phone with her when she fell."

Julia rushed to Rena's side and put an arm around her. "That must have been terrifying, but you did the right thing by calling Luke. He probably has a hundred doctors looking her over by now."

Gio frowned. "I should go, too."

Rena stood. "Gio."

Gio stopped on his way out the door and turned to look at her. "Yes?"

She wanted to tell him what Patrice had said to her. She didn't believe for a second that Patrice was actually ill, but she couldn't explain why she thought that without revealing how she felt about Nick. "Do you want me to call Nick and Max?"

"No," Gio said. "I will." He strode out the door, half dragging Julia behind him.

Rena sat back down at her desk and covered her face with both hands.

Is it a sin to not pray for someone to live?

CB

Nick sat in the main library of his mother's house with Gio and Luke. Like Gio, Nick was still dressed in his business suit. Luke was in scrubs. The only communication they'd had since they'd arrived was a nod of acknowledgment toward each other.

Luke finally broke the silence. "Does anyone know if Max is coming?"

Gio crossed his legs at his ankles and leaned back in his chair. "He's in the British Isles looking at some property. I told him we'd keep him informed and tell him if he needed to be here."

Nick asked, "Has anyone seen her yet?"

Luke folded his arms across his chest. "No one besides her physician. He turned the emergency team away. He claims this is a condition she's already under treatment for."

After running his hand through his hair, Gio said coldly, "How possible is it that this is all for show?"

Luke looked at the door with a skeptical expression. "I don't like to think badly of anyone in my profession, but her doctor is suspiciously territorial. He wouldn't let me see her or her records. Granted, I'm a surgeon, but I'm definitely qualified to recognize the severity of what he's vaguely calling episodes. So I have to ask myself, what is it he doesn't want me to see?"

Nick looked from brother to brother and said, "I'm surprised neither of you stormed in there demanding the truth."

Gio shrugged. "I don't even want to be here. I damn well don't want to be in there."

Luke shook his head and balled his hands on his knees. "I can't bring myself to accuse her of something I don't have any proof is a lie."

Nick walked over to sit at his father's old desk. "It's easy to understand why Father wanted another family, isn't it? Look at us. What is there about us that anyone could love?"

Gio stood and joined Nick. "Father loved us. He did. What happened between him and Mother didn't change how he felt for us."

"I wonder if he and Mother were ever happy," Luke asked quietly as he also joined them. "I've tried to remember a time when I saw them hold hands or laugh together. I don't think I ever did."

Nick rubbed a hand over his chin in frustration. "I'm so tired of wondering why we are the way we are. Maybe it's time to just let the past go and move on."

Gio stared straight ahead and gritted his teeth. "If only it were that easy."

"Gio, we need to talk," Nick said.

"Talk away."

"Not here."

"I'll probably be returning to Cogent for a few hours after this."

"It's not about work."

"Okay, I have all day tomorrow."

"Saturday?" Nick repeated the word, stalling. "Sunday would be better for me. I'm often tied up on Saturdays."

Luke and Gio both gave Nick a confused look, but Nick pretended not to notice. Although he had decided to tell Gio about Rena, doing it while waiting to hear about the health of their mother didn't feel right. And there was no way he was going to miss seeing Rena to break the news to Gio. Sunday or nothing.

"Fine," Gio said. "Come for dinner. Julia loves to have company."

"Where is she?" Luke asked.

"All things considered," Gio said, "we thought it was better if she didn't come."

"She and Mother are still fighting?" Nick asked.

"No," Gio said firmly. "I don't let them anywhere near each other. Julia is too important to me."

There was a time when Gio's comment would have angered Nick. He remembered accusing Gio of choosing Julia's side over their mother's. At the time he had believed Gio was wrong, but he could only imagine what his own reaction would be if he heard that his mother had threatened Rena.

A bald, heavyset doctor dressed casually in khaki pants and a polo shirt entered the library. "Your mother is feeling better now, and she'd like to see all of you."

Like men headed off to the guillotine, the three brothers followed the doctor to their mother's first-floor bedroom suite. She was dressed in a silk peignoir and sitting up beneath an ornate comforter in the middle of a king-sized bed. She lifted a hand slowly as if it were a difficult feat and beckoned her sons to her side.

"The doctor says I'm fine. I'm so sorry to have worried you."

Luke stepped forward and studied his mother's face. He lifted her hand in his, taking her pulse at the same time. "What are these episodes?"

She pulled back from him and folded both of her hands on her lap. "Talking about it only makes it more real and I don't want to get upset, so please, respect that."

Nick stood beside Luke. "It's not like I'm asking the question. Luke might know something that could help. Or"—he looked across the room at the hovering physician—"no offense, know a specialist in the field. What would it hurt to let him look over your medical records?"

Tears came to his mother's eyes. "Why do you always have to push, Nick? Can't you for once do what I'm asking of you?"

Gio took his place beside Nick. "Nick is merely concerned that you might not be getting the treatment you need. We want the best for you, Mother."

Patrice went pale and raised a shaky hand to her chest. "I'm tired. Please leave me."

Not one of the brothers moved at first. Nick wondered if Luke and Gio felt as torn as he did. Part of him wanted to call her out and demand to see her medical records. Part of him felt like the world's worst son who wanted to apologize for doubting her.

Gio was the first to speak. "Get some rest, Mother. I hope you feel better."

Luke bent and gave Patrice a kiss on the cheek. "Call me if you need me."

Nick hovered over his mother and she took his hand in hers. "Nick, I'm sorry I snapped at you. I'm not myself right now. Please, forgive me." A tear rolled down her cheek and Nick wiped it away.

"Don't cry, Mother. There is nothing to forgive." He gave her hand a final squeeze and followed his brothers out into the hallway.

Luke looked at his watch as soon as they were alone. "I hate to rush off, but I postponed a surgery and I can't push it back it again. I have to go."

Gio turned to Nick. "I'm heading back to Cogent."

Nick nodded. "Me, too. I have my own car, though."

Gio paused. "I have time now if you've changed your mind and want to talk about anything."

Having had his fill of family dealings that day, Nick said. "I'll talk to you on Sunday."

Chapter Fifteen

RENA RANG THE doorbell of the townhouse, and when no one answered she rang it again impatiently. She was hungry and tired, and she really wanted to go home. But there was someone she had to speak to before she did.

An older man, still tall and broad, answered the door with a smile. "Hello, we've met before, haven't we? Gio's secretary, Rena, right?" Rena nodded and was taken by surprise as he lifted her off the ground in a bone-crushing hug. "Welcome. The boys talk about you all the time."

"Please put me down." Once back on the ground, Rena stepped back and adjusted her clothing. She did remember meeting him. He was one of Nick's uncles.

A beautiful older woman with a warm smile stepped into the doorway and held out her hand in greeting. "Did I hear him say Rena? I'm Maddy's mother, Elise. I've been looking forward to meeting you. Come in, come in. Alessando's manners have become awful as he gotten older. Are you looking for Maddy? She's upstairs feeding Adam, but she should be down in a minute."

Rena shook her hand, then followed the couple into the foyer of Maddy's home. "This is probably a bad time. I can come back."

"No, please," Elise said warmly, "if you wait for a convenient time to visit a new mother you'll never find one. We're only here for a short time ourselves. Richard lured us over with a promise of fresh eggplant Parmesan. I don't like to tell Maddy's husband often, because it'll give him a big head, but it's as good as Alessandro's mother used to make."

Alessandro patted his heart and spoke to the heavens. "Mama, she doesn't remember your sauce like I do."

Elise laughed and told Rena in a confidential tone, "I do." She motioned toward the living room. "Please, join us for coffee. Or stay for dinner if you're hungry. We have more than enough."

Rena reluctantly sat and accepted a cup. She'd come with the intention of giving Maddy a piece of her mind about her loose tongue, but there was also something very tempting about meeting one of the infamous Andrade uncles. Rena knew the stories of Alessandro and Victor well. She'd grown up hearing about their private island near Italy, and then had witnessed the fallout amongst the family after Nick's father died. A situation which had gotten worse when the uncles had sold the island, which should have been Gio's inheritance, to a stranger. Gio had come back from a family wedding several months ago and had simply said that not everything he'd thought about his uncles had been true. Luke had told Rena that Gio and one of his cousins now co-owned the island, an agreement the family had come to in the spirit of reunification.

Alessandro was one of the uncles Patrice had spent a lifetime raising her sons to distrust. Rena hadn't expected to meet them, but she considered herself a good judge of character. She welcomed the opportunity to meet the people Patrice said had never accepted her.

She tested the waters, hoping to prompt a reaction that would reveal their true nature. "I'll be honest, I'm not here because I'm happy with Maddy."

Alessandro sighed and took a seat beside Rena. "What did my darling daughter do?"

"It's more about what she didn't do. I told her something in confidence and she told others about it."

Alessandro nodded with understanding and called to Elise, who was walking back into the room with sugar for Rena's coffee: "She's upset because Maddy's telling everyone that she's seeing Nick."

Rena covered her eyes with one hand and swore.

Elise sat beside Rena and touched her shoulder gently. "I told her it was none of her business, but Maddy thinks everyone can benefit from a little loving nudge. She's not doing it to hurt you."

Raising her head, Rena said, "How do I stop her?"

Alessandro shrugged a broad shoulder. "How do you tell the leaves not to fall from the trees? It's her nature."

Rena looked back and forth between Alessandro and Elise. They weren't angry with her for having an issue with their daughter, nor defending Maddy. They appeared comfortable with themselves and their faults. Although that realization wasn't helpful to her situation, it didn't make them people Rena could imagine spending a lifetime despising. There had to be something she was missing. Had they hurt Patrice and been as careless about her pain? There was only one way to know. "So, you don't care how much your daughter hurts others? It's her nature?"

Alessandro sat forward. "Maddy would never intentionally hurt anyone. She's all heart."

Elise leaned in, concerned. "Rena, I'm sure she has no idea this is bothering you as much as it is. I'll talk to her with you. She means well, but sometimes she crosses the line."

"Who crosses what line?" Maddy asked as she breezed into the room with a young baby in her arms.

Alessandro stood and took Adam from her. He cooed his reprimand while making funny faces at his grandchild. "Madison, you owe Rena an apology for telling everyone something she told you not to." The baby gurgled up at the large man. He tickled his neck with one finger and said, "Tell Mommy to apologize, Adam. You think it's funny?" He tickled the baby again. "It's not funny."

Elise put her hands on her hips and raised her eyebrows at her daughter.

Maddy smiled sheepishly. "I didn't tell that many people."

Rena stared her down. "I asked you not to tell anyone."

"Nick is lucky I haven't seen him yet," Alessandro said. "Andrades treat their women better than he's treating you, Rena. One day you'll be grateful Maddy made him step up and act like the man he should be."

"Who did you tell?" Rena demanded.

Maddy didn't meet her eyes. "My parents don't count. I tell them everything. Same thing with Richard. A wife doesn't keep secrets from husband."

Rena waited.

"Does Nicole count? She's family, and she also had a secret relationship that turned out well after the dust settled. So, I knew she would understand."

Gritting her teeth, Rena held her silence, knowing that Maddy would keep confessing as long as the pressure remained.

"I may have told Abby Corisi and her sister, Lil, because we have a bet going about who is the best matchmaker, and I wanted to claim you as a point for Nicole and me."

Rena raised an eyebrow.

"Okay, and I also told Nick's mother, because she wanted to know why he was too busy to see her lately."

Rena stood. "That's where you went too far. Don't tell Patrice another word about me. You understand? Nothing. By talking to her, you may have ruined everything."

Maddy's expression revealed her confusion. "I'm sorry. I thought she'd be pleased he'd found someone nice."

Elise looked at her husband quickly. "Maddy, I didn't know you were talking to Patrice."

Maddy swung to face her parents, her confusion growing. "I have been for a while now. I thought I'd told you that."

Alessandro's expression darkened. "No, you didn't."

Elise wrung her hands in front of her. "Maddy, don't go see her anymore. She's not a happy woman."

"Of course she's not happy," Maddy defended, "she's very ill. Which seems like a reason I should go see her. She loves hearing about the family."

Rena muttered, "I'm sure she does."

Maddy threw up her hands in frustration. "She's an old woman."

Elise protested, "She's not much older than us."

"And from what I hear, maybe not as ill as she'd like people to think." Alessandro handed his grandchild to his wife and walked over to his daughter. "Maddy, not everyone is as good of a person as you are. Some don't deserve your trust."

Rena put aside how she felt about Maddy's betrayal long enough to agree. "You don't know what Patrice is capable of. Don't give her more ammunition to use against us."

Shaking her head, Maddy said, "She's not like that."

Rena weighed her options, then said, "Did you tell her about Julia? Because Patrice threatened to break them up before the wedding. And she almost succeeded. She says she has photos of Nick and me that's she's going to send to the tabloids. She's using you, Maddy. Stop helping her."

Maddy brought her hands up to her mouth, and her eyes shone with tears. "That can't be true." She looked to her parents for support. "This has to be a misunderstanding. Right? Why wouldn't she want her sons to be happy?"

Elise spoke softly her husband. "Alessandro, maybe it's time to tell Maddy what we know."

"No," Alessandro said with finality. "The past is dead, gone with George. I will not discuss this further. Maddy, you are forbidden to visit with Patrice again. Rena, I'm sorry for the trouble my daughter has caused you. Now, I suggest we eat the food Richard has prepared for us before it gets cold and put this topic to rest."

Rena walked up to Alessandro and said, "What do you know that you're not saying? What happened between your family and Patrice?"

Alessandro turned and walked out to the foyer, saying, "You're always welcome here, Rena, but right now I think you should go."

Following Alessandro, Rena implored one last time: "You don't have to tell me, but her sons deserve to know the truth."

The older man looked away, and Rena stepped outside. A moment later, Maddy was standing at the door calling her name. Rena turned.

"Rena, I'm sorry I said anything. That's it. I'm just sorry."

Rena shook her head. "Just don't say anything to anyone. Stay out of it. You're making it worse."

"But—" Maddy started.

Her husband joined her at the door, pulling her gently to his side. "Maddy, let her go."

She gazed up at her husband and said, "Richard, you don't know what I did."

He kissed her forehead. "I know you well enough to guess. I also know you need to listen to what your friend is asking you to do. If she wants your help, she'll ask you for it, *non?*"

"Will you, Rena? Will you call me if you need me?"

The sweetness of Maddy's plea made it impossible for Rena to remain angry with her. She would never again speak frankly in front of her, but Maddy, as Elise claimed, meant well. Rena wished she could say the same about everyone in Nick's family. "Sure, Maddy."

Rena slid into her car feeling she'd learned much more than she'd expected to from the visit, but that she'd left with even more questions. She called her own parents on the drive back.

"Mom, I love you and Dad, and I am so grateful for both of you."

"Rena?" her mother's voice echoed through the car speaker. "Are you okay?"

"Yes. No." Rena paused. "I don't know, Mom. All I do know is I will never take you and Dad for granted again."

"Do you want me to drive into the city tonight, honey?"

"No, Mom, I'm fine. I just wanted to hear your voice."

"You sound upset. Does this have anything to do with Nick?"

On the thirty-minute drive back to her house, Rena took a page out of Maddy's book and told her mother everything.

❧

Some days are longer than others. Dressed in cotton shorts and a pink T-shirt, Rena plopped down on her couch, picked up her television remote, then put it down beside her unused.

She closed her eyes and ran through the day's events. By Andrade standards, her mother was a saint, but that didn't mean she'd kept her opinion to herself when Rena told her she'd been seeing Nick secretly, and how photos of them together might surface. Rena quickly moved on to how heartbreaking it was to spend time with Nick and his dysfunctional family.

It was only when her mother circled back to what Rena was doing with Nick that their conversation became tense. *How do you explain hot Saturday sex trumping common sense?* Rena didn't bother. She kept her answers simple and vague. "I know what I'm doing, Mom. I don't have expectations of this going anywhere. We're just having fun."

That had been the wrong thing to say.

Her mother had expressed her concern again and again until Rena had lost her patience. "Mom, I'm not asking if you agree with what I'm doing. And I don't need your permission to keep seeing Nick. I'm happy with things the way they are. I called you because I'm afraid everything is about to change and I don't want to lose Nick."

"Do you even have him?" her mother had asked.

"Yes," Rena had replied angrily. "I have him in my life the only way that makes sense. And I've been happier like this than I can ever remember being. Can you try to understand that?"

"I can try," her mother had said sadly. "I just want more for you, Rena. You deserve better."

"You don't get it."

"Oh, honey. I do. I want to tell you that you can have what you want and not ever pay the price for it, but that's not reality. The choices you make directly determine the path your life will take. I don't want you to look back at this time and regret that you accepted less than you should have."

What did I think my mother would say? Keep screwing that guy we all warned you to stay away from. Or: Here, I have a magical wand that will make all the issues with his family go away.

There had to be a way that things could stay as they were. Maybe Patrice wouldn't follow through with her threats. *I guess I can hope she's so ill she'll forget what she said.* Maddy now understood how important it was that she stop talking about Rena and Nick. So there was a slim chance that nothing had to change.

Tomorrow is Saturday.

Nick hadn't called to cancel their date, so as far as she knew they were still on for a day in the Poconos. They'd decided to pretend they were newlyweds and stay in one of the hotel's rooms that had a large champagne-glass bathtub. It was only a couple of hours drive away, but they'd decided to travel by Cessna plane. Nick had a pilot's license, and it gave them the freedom to be spontaneous with their time.

Unless his mother really is sick and he hasn't had time to call and cancel.

Does it make me a bad person that I'm hoping she had a quick recovery, just so my plans for tomorrow don't change?

It is Patrice.

The doorbell rang and Rena groaned. It rang again and Rena pulled herself off the couch. *I swear if it's Maddy I cannot be held responsible for losing my temper. I'm done with that whole side of the family for today.*

Rena looked through the peephole, then swung the door open. "Nick? What are you doing here?"

"Can I come in?"

"Sure." She closed the door behind him.

"It's been one hell of a day."

Tell me about it, Rena thought sarcastically. Rena wrapped her arms around her waist. "How is your mother?"

Nick took a step toward Rena. "I don't want to talk about her." There was something different about Nick. Rena couldn't quite pin it down. He wasn't playful like he was during their Saturday dates. He had a predatory gleam in his eyes, and it made Rena retreat each time he advanced.

"What do you want to talk about?" Rena asked, bumping into the edge of her coffee table as she backed away from him.

"I didn't come here to talk." He reached for Rena, but she sidestepped him and moved so that the couch was between them.

Rena raised a hand. "Nick, we can't do this."

He dropped his coat behind him. "Yes, we can."

"Okay, let me rephrase that. Nick, we're not doing this."

He pulled his shirt free from his slacks, unbuttoned it slowly, and dropped it beside him without taking his eyes off her. Rena's heart began to race wildly in her chest. The entire day had felt out of control, and now Nick was testing their arrangement. She couldn't lose control of this, too. He undid his belt and the top of his pants, and stepped out of his shoes and clothing in one smooth move. He dropped them on the couch between them. His full state of arousal left little doubt as to why Nick had come over.

Rena grabbed his pants and threw them at him. "Put your pants back on."

Nick caught them easily and dropped them beside him on the floor. "No. I've been thinking about you all day and I don't want to wait until tomorrow. Admit it, Rena, you don't want to either."

"What I want is for you to get dressed and leave. This is my home. You're not supposed to be here."

Unashamed of his nudity or his arousal, Nick looked around the room. "Do you have someone here?"

Rena stomped her foot in frustration. It was taking all of her restraint to hold to the rules they'd set in the beginning, but it was only because of those rules that Rena felt safe with Nick. He could only hurt her if she fell for him, and she had no intention of doing that. "It's none of your business if I do."

With catlike swiftness, Nick moved around the couch and grabbed Rena's forearm with enough force that she winced. "Do you or don't you have anyone here?"

Rena pulled at her arm, but he refused to release it. With her lips pressed together angrily, she said, "Of course I don't. That's not the point. You don't have the right to ask me if I do."

He frowned at her. "You will not have other men in your life, Rena. Not while you're with me."

Rena tugged to free her arm again. She didn't like how standing so close to Nick was affecting her. No matter what her brain said, her body was readying itself for the pleasure it knew it could find with him. Her panties were soaking wet in anticipation, and she hated that her nipples were pressing against her thin shirt. "You're hurting me," she growled.

Nick looked down at his hand and instantly released her. "Sorry."

His apology would have seemed much more sincere if he hadn't been waving his excited cock at her when he said it. Rena glanced down at it and licked her bottom lip. A cock she knew the taste and feel of. She wanted to reach out and stroke it in the way she'd learned Nick liked the most. She wanted to sink to her knees before him, take him in her mouth, and drive him out of his mind, until all he could do was call her name and beg her not to stop.

But not on Friday.

"Please leave, Nick."

Nick rubbed a hand across his chin and said, "I don't want to."

Rena waved at his erection and said, "I can see that, but that doesn't change how I feel."

He stepped closer to her, and Rena inhaled loudly as the tip of his cock brushed her leg. She refused to look down at it again. "How do you feel, Rena?" He ran one finger down the side of her neck and traced her collarbone, then took her excited nipple between his thumb and forefinger and rolled it gently. "Are you wet for me already? My guess is yes."

Rena was going to step back, but Nick held her in place by wrapping one arm around her waist. "Don't, Nick."

"Don't what?" Nick asked and ran his free hand down her flat stomach toward the waistband of her shorts. He boldly slid a hand underneath the fabric, then beneath her panties to cup her sex. "Don't do this?" He dipped one finger inside her, plunging it deeply, then withdrawing it. "Or this." He rubbed his thumb back and forth over her clit.

Rena closed her eyes and gasped for air. She gripped one of his bare shoulders with her hand and cried out with pleasure when his mouth settled on her breast and suckled her through the material of her shirt.

"I can stop if you want me to, but do you want me to, Rena? I don't think you do." He pulled her shorts and panties down her legs with a move so strong it was almost painful. She stood before him, unable to tell him to leave again, unwilling to admit she wanted him to stay. He pulled her shirt up over her head, and they stood there in a naked and highly charged sexual standoff.

Rena said nothing as he ran his hands over her, slowly exploring her body as he had many times before, but this time his touch was rougher. The determination in his eyes set Rena on fire. She wanted to resist him, but she also wanted him to take what she normally gave him.

He turned her around, and pressing firmly on her back, bent her over the arm of the couch. He held her there while he ran his other hand back and forth over her exposed sex. With one of his feet, he moved hers farther apart, exposing her more fully to him.

Then he sunk to his knees behind her and buried his face in her sex. His tongue dove within her then withdrew, only to plunge in again. He kneaded her ass with one hand while his other worked its rhythmic magic on her nub.

He lapped at her until she was whimpering from the pleasure of it, then moved to lick the inside of her thighs. He nipped at her buttock, then kissed his way up her spine. He paused, and Rena heard the sound of him opening a condom package. She clenched in anticipation.

He rubbed the tip of his dick up and down her sex, following the path his tongue had taken. Then he reached forward, took Rena's hair in one hand and pulled her head back until she was arched before him. He laid his other hand on her hip and leaned down to whisper in her ear.

"You're mine, Rena. Not just on Saturday. You're mine any day I want you. Say it."

Rena shook her head. Nick drove his cock deeply inside her.

"I'm not playing by your rules anymore, Rena." He pulled himself out and thrust back into her as if driving his point home. "And if you do have anyone else in your life, get rid of him now, before I do."

Rena would have protested, but the feel of him above her, inside her, hitting her G-spot with every deep thrust was more than she could fight against. As he pounded into her, heat spread through her with such intensity that she finally cried out, "Yes," again and again. She slumped forward over the couch, and he climaxed soon after her.

He withdrew, picked her up, and carried her to her bedroom. He gently pulled back the bedsheets, laid her down beneath them, and slid in beside her. When he tucked her against his side and kissed her temple, Rena rolled over and angrily pushed at him. "Stop it," she snapped. "You're ruining everything."

CB

Nick easily held Rena to him. He'd never realized how adorable she looked when she was irritated. He bent and kissed her gently even as she glared at him. She kept her lips pressed angrily together. He rolled over, pinning her beneath him, and smoothed the hair out of her face. "What is going in that head of yours? I thought what we just had was amazing."

Rena stopped struggling and looked away. "It was. It always is, but not here and not on a Friday. You can't stay."

"Are you fucking serious?" Nick laughed. When she tensed beneath him instead of laughing too, he stopped abruptly and said, "You are serious."

"We can see each other tomorrow."

Nick looked at the clock beside Rena's bed. "It'll be tomorrow in two hours. It doesn't make sense to go home only to come right back."

"We have an agreement. You agreed not to do this."

"Well, I'm amending our agreement. Rule number five point two four will now read, 'If sex commences on Friday after eight p.m., the no-overnight statute will be null and void from that point onward.' "

"Don't make fun of me, Nick."

"Then don't be ridiculous. I'm here tonight for one reason and one reason only—I want to be with you. Yes, what we just did on your couch was fantastic, but I also wanted to talk to you. We don't have a lot of time alone."

Rena scoffed at the idea. "We're together every Saturday."

"Not like this," Nick said and nuzzled his face in her hair. "We're always running off somewhere, and not that that isn't incredible, but it doesn't leave us much time to talk."

"You want to talk? Isn't that a woman's line?"

Nick took her chin in his hand and turned her face so that she was forced to meet his eyes. "Now who is making fun of whom?"

Rena looked unhappily cornered. "Nick. I understand today was a tough day for you and if you want to talk, let's get dressed and go somewhere. But I can't do this." She waved one hand in a circle beside him.

Nick was momentarily at a loss for what to say and, in that pause, Rena continued, "I'm sorry. I know that was insensitive." She let out a long breath as if seeking inner calm. "How is your mother?"

"She was fine when we left her."

"I'm glad. Was everyone there? Gio, Luke, Max?"

Nick sighed and rolled onto his side. "Max, the lucky bastard, was out of the country."

"But Gio and Luke were there?"

"Yes, we went in to see Mother together."

"Good."

"Luke said you were on the phone with her when she had her episode. What were you talking about?"

Rena looked away again. "Nothing important."

"Don't lie to me, Rena. Did you call her or did she call you?"

"She called me."

"I didn't realize the two of you were that close."

"We're not."

"What did she do, threaten you like she threatened Julia?" Nick was joking, but when Rena looked away again all humor left him. "She fucking did, didn't she?"

Rena shifted toward the edge of the bed, but Nick stopped her by throwing an arm around her waist. The act sent the sheet flying off her, and her glorious breasts bounced free as she pushed at his arm and tried to rise from the bed. "It was nothing."

A slow, burning anger began to build within Nick. He didn't doubt Rena for a second. She had never lied to him. He'd found his truth.

In that moment, so much that had confused him became clear. Things his mother had said to him over the years made sense now when he viewed them as the words of a bitter and vindictive woman. She'd blackened his opinion of Gio with her stories of how he had greedily taken control of Cogent. She's kept up her version of the villainous Andrade clan when Nick only remembered them warmly welcoming him.

As with a rotten onion, the more memories Nick peeled back, the more vileness he revealed. *I've been looking for the answers when they were obvious all along.*

Patrice was at the heart of everything that was wrong with his family. She was the reason her sons didn't trust each other. He thought back to all the times she'd encouraged him to walk away from the family business, and it infuriated him that he'd allowed himself to be manipulated for so long.

He looked down at Rena. "Tell me exactly what my mother said," he ordered.

Rena put a hand over the one that gripped her side. "Ow, you're pinching me."

He instantly rubbed his hand soothingly over the area, but he didn't release her. He sat up on his knees and pulled her to a kneeling position in front of him. "I need the truth. Tell me what you know."

"It's not pretty. I'm not even sure you'll believe me. I barely believe it myself."

Exposed to her more than just physically, Nick had never felt closer to Rena. "I trust you, more than I trust my own family. And I will never allow anyone to hurt you, Rena. Especially not one of them."

Rena chewed her bottom lip, then met his eyes worriedly. "Your mother doesn't want you working at Cogent, and she's willing to do whatever it takes to make sure you don't make it there. She said she has pictures of us she'll give to the tabloids if I don't encourage you to quit. Nick, I don't care about photos. My father wouldn't be happy, but it doesn't scare me. What did scare me was when she said she knew just how to sabotage you. She said if I didn't help her she'd get you to drink again, and you'd get yourself fired from Cogent."

Nick didn't doubt Rena, but it took a few moments for her words to fully sink in. "Why doesn't she want me to work at Cogent?"

Rena shrugged. "I don't know."

"Does Gio know what she said?"

"No, well... maybe. I told your uncle, Alessandro." Rena tapped her forehead in self-reprimand. "I probably shouldn't have said it in front of Maddy. Everyone on the East Coast might know by now. I'm sorry. I wasn't thinking. It's just that Maddy was telling everyone about us. I went over to tell her to stop and then I found out she was telling your mother everything and I freaked."

"You told Maddy about us?"

Rena nodded.

"Anyone else?"

"My mother knows."

Nick rubbed Rena's arms. As much as his stomach was still churning from what he'd discovered about his family, he also felt a certain amount of satisfaction from knowing that Rena was telling people they were together. "What did your mother say when you told her about us?"

Rena rolled her eyes. "What everyone else says about the idea of us together, but she doesn't understand that I'm okay with how we are. My mother thinks I'll do something foolish like fall for you, but that's why we keep to our agreement. That's why we have rules."

Nick frowned. "I thought the rules were a game. You know, to keep it fun and exciting."

Rena waved her hands emphatically in front of her as she spoke. "That too, but it also keeps me grounded in what is possible between us."

Nick lowered his hands. "And that is?"

Rena slapped a hand on her bare leg. "Nick, we both know you don't do relationships. You've never lied about that. I'd be a fool if I thought a little sex with me could change your nature. That's how people get hurt—they have crazy expectations that the other person can't live up to. I wanted to be with you, Nick, and I had to find a way to be okay with who you are, not who I wanted you to be. And I did. What we're doing works. That's why you can't sleep over. I know it's silly, but our Saturdays together are a treat I give myself. Like a vacation. You know it's not forever, but you enjoy it while you're there."

Nick folded his arms in front of him. "Saturdays are really about keeping your expectations purely about sex, because that's the only area in which you feel I won't disappoint you?"

"It sounds really bad when you put it that way. I didn't say that."

Nick stood beside the bed. "Yes, you did."

Rena scrambled to stand beside him. "Nick, let's start over. I explained it all wrong."

Nick held up a hand to halt her from saying more. "Save it. I couldn't stomach hearing it twice." He walked back into her living room not caring if Rena followed him, but she did. He pulled on his pants and shrugged back into his shirt without speaking to her. He was lacing up the second of his shoes when she spoke again.

"I'm sorry, Nick. I shouldn't have said it the way I did."

The sad look in her eyes only confused Nick more. He wasn't angry with her—how could he be? He straightened and took in the beauty of her standing before him. Any self-consciousness she might have had about her nudity was overshadowed by the concern she had for his feelings. Which made what she'd said about him that much more bitter of a pill to swallow. "Rena, I've always admired your honesty. Thank you for telling me exactly what I needed to hear."

Rena stepped in front of him just before he reached the door. "Will I see you tomorrow?"

He pulled her into his arms and gave her a tender, emotional kiss that left them both shaken, then set her back from him. "No," he said simply and let himself out of her house, closing the door firmly behind him.

Chapter Sixteen

RENA DIDN'T LEAVE her house on Saturday. She waited for Nick to change his mind and call her, or simply show up at her door. As hour after hour passed, she sought for something to distract herself. She emptied the cabinets in her kitchen, then reorganized them. But when she finished, instead of enjoying the calm such a task normally brought her, she felt profoundly sad.

One tear escaped, rolling down her cheek as she stood there in the silence of her kitchen, the only sound her own ragged breathing.

Nick isn't coming today.

No one had to try to break us up. I did it myself.

She played and replayed their final conversation in her head. *He came to me because he was upset and wanted to be with me. And what do I do? I tell him horrendous things about his family and then make it sound like I don't care about him either.*

He must feel so alone right now.

And it's my fault.

She dug her cell phone out of her pocket and dialed Nick's number. Her call went directly to his voice mail—just like all the calls she'd placed since the night before. She sent him a text: **Are you okay?**

He didn't respond.

She sunk to the floor and sat with her phone on her lap, waiting for the beep that accompanied an incoming message. As the silence dragged on, Rena's eyes filled with tears that she couldn't stop. One shallow sob led to a deeper one until they wracked her body and she wanted nothing more than to curl up in a corner and cry until the ache in her heart eased.

Blinded by the tears, she fumbled with her phone and dialed the number of the only person she knew would understand how she felt. She took several calming breaths while the phone rang, but started to cry again when her mother picked up. "Mom?" she asked in a tight, tear-laden voice.

"Rena? What's the matter? Are you hurt?"

Rena sniffed. "Mom, you were right about everything. I should have listened to you. I thought if I protected myself, it wouldn't hurt this much. I was wrong. Nick and I broke up and it hurts so much. I would come to you, but I don't think I can drive. Can you come here, Mom?"

"Oh, baby, don't go anywhere. I'm on my way."

A few minutes later Rena heard the outer door of her house open and close. "Rena?" Kane's voice bellowed through her house.

No.

Rena pulled herself off the floor and wiped away her tears with a paper towel. She blew her nose in a second one, then tried to cool her face with a third. She cleared her throat, stayed facing the sink, and called out, "In here."

"Mom told Dad she was coming to the city because you're upset. Dad asked me to drop by. What happened?"

Rena turned with a wet paper towel still in hand and leaned back against the sink. "Nothing I can talk to you about, Kane. That's why I called Mom."

Kane's expression darkened as he studied Rena's face. "You can tell me anything."

Rena looked up at the ceiling before meeting Kane's eyes. "You say that, Kane, but you'll only hear what you want to hear if I try to talk to you about this. And honestly, I don't want to feel worse than I do right now, and you would make me feel worse, even if you didn't mean to. So, Kane, can you just leave me alone until after I talk to Mom? I really can't handle you right now."

"Rena, did someone hurt you? Tell me who and I'll..."

"See why I can't talk to you? No one hurt me, Kane. I did this."

"Whatever it is, Rena, I'll make it right. Just tell me what happened."

Fresh tears started to spill down Rena's cheeks. "You can't fix this for me, Kane. Could you stop thinking it's your job to protect me and just listen to me for once?"

Kane walked over and leaned against the counter beside his sister. "Are you pregnant?"

Rena rolled her eyes.

Kane sighed. "I'm trying, Rena. You look like you just lost your best friend. What the hell happened?"

Rena wiped the tears from her cheeks and said, "That's exactly what just happened."

Kane slumped with relief. "That's it? Thank God."

Rena glared at him.

Kane pulled her to his side for a hug. "I'm not belittling what you're going through. I just imagined at least ten possibilities I couldn't live with." He let out a long breath. "So, who did you have a fight with?"

"I didn't fight with anyone," Rena said sadly. "I just disappointed someone I care about very much in a way I never meant to."

"You?" Kane pulled back and raised one eyebrow in doubt. "The person who is always trying to make sure everyone else is happy? You could never disappoint anyone."

"You'd be surprised, Kane."

"I'm here if you want to talk about it, Rena. I won't say a thing. I'll just listen. I promise."

"There is a lot of crap going on right now, Kane, and I could use your advice with some of it, but I'm not a little girl anymore. You don't have to run up to the bully in the playground and punch him out for me. If I tell you what's going on, I want you to listen to the whole story and then do nothing if that's what I ask you to do. Can you promise me that?"

"I don't know."

Rena looked up at her brother. "Swear to me you won't say or do anything. If I tell you what happened and you make this situation worse, I won't talk to you again, Kane. Not about anything that matters."

Kane frowned. "I promise to only get as involved as you ask me to. Now, tell me, what happened."

Rena squared her shoulders and said, "Nick and I just broke up."

⚃

Nick had turned his phone off as soon as Rena's first call had come in. He still wasn't ready to deal with the emotions their last conversation had stirred in him. He'd spent the night walking the city's streets, not wanting to go back to his hotel room but also not wanting to head to a club, as he once would have. He'd started off feeling angry at Rena for dismissing him, especially after he'd turned to her for comfort as he'd never done with others. For the first time in his life, he wanted to wake up next to the same person every day. And he wanted that someone to be Rena. It hadn't been easy to hear she'd invested as much emotion in him as she would have a trip to Disney.

Not that he blamed her. His track record with women spoke for itself. What had she said—she'd be a fool to think sex with her could change him? While walking around the city, he'd thought about how he could have responded instead of just walking away.

He could have told her it wasn't the sex that had changed him, it was all the times they met in the hallway at work and talked about nothing. He looked forward to seeing her and doing absolutely nothing more than he'd ever looked forward to doing anything with anyone.

What had changed him? The way she smiled at him when she thought he wasn't looking. The way she defended him when she thought he couldn't hear her. Even those damn birthday cards. What kind of person keeps sending cards when the recipient never acknowledges them?

Rena. The most warmhearted, loyal woman he'd ever met.

A woman who had very sincerely told him he was good enough for sex and nothing more. The worst part was, when he looked at himself through her eyes, he had to agree with her.

As he'd continued to walk down the artificially lit streets of a city that never slept, Nick had admitted he was also angry that Rena had forced him to reassess everything he thought he knew about himself and his family.

He'd spent a good hour hating his mother and blaming her for everything that was or had ever been wrong with his life. He'd wasted some time pondering what had happened to make her the type of mother who would hurt her own children if they stood between her and what she wanted.

Finally, he'd stopped when he caught his reflection in a department store window. How Rena viewed him was a consequence of how he had lived his life until that point. He could have made better choices. He'd looked into his own eyes and acknowledged what he had been denying until then.

All of this is equally my fault.

He saw then that his mother had played on his insecurities and his pride. Both traits had been weaknesses, just as destructive to his life as his love of alcohol had been. It was time to leave them behind, as he had the bottle. Continuing down the street, he'd begun to see patterns in his life that he wanted—no needed—to break.

As the sun came up, Nick realized his seemingly random walk had led him to the high-rise building where Gio and Julia lived. He announced himself to the doorman, who placed a quick phone call upstairs. Then Nick was directed to the elevator that served his brother's penthouse.

With his wet hair slicked back, Gio answered the door in a thick white bathrobe. Julia, also dripping wet, stood behind him dressed in similar attire. Gio said gruffly, "I hope this is important. Julia and I were—" He stopped there.

Julia added sweetly and blushed, "Showering."

Nick ran a hand through his already mussed hair. "Can I come in?"

Gio opened the door wider, then told Nick to give them a few minutes to get dressed. Gio returned in lounge pants and a T-shirt. Julia had thrown on yoga pants and a sweatshirt. Still dressed in yesterday's suit, Nick looked like a man on a walk of shame home—which would have been accurate if he'd had more than a hotel room to return to.

Nick shrugged awkwardly. "I probably should have called before coming over."

Gio didn't correct him.

Julia smiled at him again. "Would you like a cup of coffee, Nick?"

Nick waved off the idea. "No, don't bother. I'm fine. This won't take long."

Gio shrugged in resignation and sat down. "You might as well have some, Nick. You look like shit, and we're already dressed."

Julia leaned over the back of the couch, wrapped her arms around Gio's shoulders, and kissed his neck. Gio smiled and leaned into her caress while warmly rubbing her arm. Their obvious affection for each other was touching to witness. Julia straightened and said, "I'll make a nice big breakfast, which will give the two of you time to chat." She started to walk toward the kitchen, then turned back and said, "I'm glad you're here, Nick. Gio is, too."

When she was out of earshot, Nick said, "She's really sweet, isn't she?"

Gio's expression remained guarded. "Cut the shit, Nick. What are you doing here? What do you want?"

Nick sat in the chair across from Gio. "I need to ask you a question, and I don't want you to sugarcoat your answer. Give me the unfiltered truth."

Gio rubbed the back of his neck like the idea gave him a headache, then said, "Ask away."

"Do you consider me a full partner at Cogent?"

Gio clenched his hand on his lap. "That's an interesting question. If you're looking to cash out your share, we don't have the liquid assets right now to do it."

Nick sat forward. "I'm not talking about money, Gio. I'm asking if you're including me in what's really going on there, or if you're feeding me projects that don't really matter just to keep me occupied."

"What do you want me to say, Nick? You want to take over one of the big contracts? Is that what you're looking for? I can't simply hand those to you. I won't risk the future of Cogent just because your ego needs bolstering. You'll get those contracts when you're ready for them."

Nick ran his hand through his hair again. "This isn't about that either."

"Then for God's sake, Nick, don't dance around whatever it is you're trying to say. It's too fucking early in the morning for me to play twenty questions with you."

"Gio, I know there is something going on that has you worried. I don't know what news came in last week, but it wasn't good, was it?"

Gio took a deep breath before answering. "No, it wasn't."

"What did you find out?"

"I'm handling it," Gio growled and stood.

Nick also surged to his feet and blocked his brother's path. "Alone. Like you handled everything that happened when Father died."

"Yes."

"But you don't have to. I'm right here, Gio. You said you wanted me working at the company with you. You said we'd run it together. If something is jeopardizing it, tell me. I can help."

Gio shook his head. "Nick, this isn't like a broken fax machine or a stubborn politician. I need to handle this one."

"Because you're trying to protect me, or because you don't believe I'm as committed to Cogent's success as you are? You may have worked there longer, but I am now just as invested as you are. If it's a problem with raising capital, use *my* trust fund. I'm not going anywhere this time, Gio. I'm all in. But you're going to have to trust me."

Gio stared at Nick for a long, silent moment before saying, "It's something I thought I had resolved a long time ago. I found the issue when I first took over the company. Money we should have had was missing. Large amounts of money. That's why we were teetering. Someone had falsified accounting records to try to cover it. Bills were recorded as having been paid that weren't. Big payouts. I couldn't find who was responsible. I was afraid it was Father and that if the truth came out our family would be ruined. So I covered it up by pouring money into the company. My name is all over enough false documents to incriminate me if it were ever investigated."

"Why would anyone investigate it now, after all this time?"

"I don't know, but I received an anonymous letter last week from someone who said if I didn't pay them twenty million dollars they were going to leak the original accounting records, along with an accusation that I was somehow involved in the original disappearance of the money."

Nick silently absorbed the enormity of what Gio was saying, even as his brother continued to explain. "Nick, our stocks would plummet if such an accusation became public—especially if it sparked an investigation. Cogent is doing well, but we're extended pretty thinly right now. We could lose everything."

"We won't," Nick said, and as he voiced the words his confidence grew. "You're not alone this time, remember? I know people who could help us solve this. We'll find out who wrote that letter."

Gio's house phone rang. He picked it up, listened, and looked across the room at Nick with an odd expression on his face. He hung up and said, "Kane's on his way up. He wanted to know if you were here."

Oh, shit.

As Nick often did, he made a joke in the face of something unpleasant. "Did he sound homicidal?"

Gio's eyes narrowed, and he took an aggressive step toward Nick. "Should he?"

Shrugging, Nick said, "I did have one other topic I wanted to discuss with you, but it can wait until after breakfast—if I live through it."

"Tell me you didn't sleep with Rena," Gio growled.

"There was no sleeping involved, ever," Nick said then, instantly regretted not answering more seriously when Gio's face turned bright red. "Gio, it's not what you think. Well, it's pretty close to your worst fears, but I really care about her." Gio took another angry step toward Nick, and Nick backed away while continuing to voice the thoughts that were coming to him. "I really care about Rena. I think I love her. Oh, my God. I think I love her."

Gio grabbed Nick by the front of his shirt and hauled him forward onto his tiptoes. The doorbell rang, but both ignored it. "Get that fucking stupid smile off your face, Nick. I can't believe I trusted you with her."

Julia swept into the room, paused beside them, and said, "Gio, put your brother down, someone is at the door."

Gio released Nick with an audible snarl.

Nick suddenly didn't care that Gio was upset with him. He couldn't stop smiling.

Julia opened the door and looked from Kane to Nick.

Nick pointed at Kane for emphasis and said loudly, "I love your sister."

Kane strode up to Nick until they were nose to nose. "That will not save you, Nick. Gio, I am not allowed to tell your brother how much I want to wrap my hands around his scrawny little neck until he turns purple. I promised my sister I wouldn't get involved, so I'm not here. I am not threatening to rip your brother limb from limb if he doesn't find a way to stop your mother from leaking photos of him with Rena to the tabloids."

Unfazed by Kane, Nick waved a hand at Gio. "Shit, the photos. That's the other reason I came here. We have to stop Mother. I don't know what exactly she has photos of, but Rena and I have done some pretty wild things that you wouldn't want made public."

"I don't care what I promised, I'm going to kill him," Kane declared.

Julia linked arms with him and cheerfully said, "Let's have breakfast first. Everyone's in a better mood on a full stomach. I made plenty. It's already set out. Come on." When no one moved, she looked across the room at her fiancé and prompted, "Gio, ask everyone to join us in the other room."

Gio threw an angry hand up in the air and started walking toward the kitchen.

Julia put her other arm through Nick's. With a smile on her face, she threatened both him and Kane. "I am not above throwing either one of you out. You're not animals. You're grown men, and you will act like gentlemen when you're in my house. Am I clear? Gio has had an awful week, and he doesn't need whatever drama the two of you brought here this morning. You're a family. Work it out."

Gio turned as he approached the kitchen door. His expression changed as he caught the tail end of his fiancée taking his brother and best friend to task. He actually smiled.

The doorbell rang again. While Gio strode off to answer it, Nick smiled down at Julia. "Whatever you say, Julia. You're my favorite sister-in-law."

Julia blushed. "Gio and I aren't married yet."

"You will be soon enough," Nick said.

Kane grumbled. "If you think being nice to her will save your—"

Nick dropped Julia's arm. "Kane, I understand how you feel. I'll admit I sometimes make light of things I probably shouldn't. It's part of my charm. But I was serious when I said I love your sister. I'll do whatever it takes to protect her, even if it's from my own family."

Kane held Nick's eyes, obviously not won over yet.

Nick continued, "And I'll stay away from her, not because you want me to, but because I want her to be happy. Whether she dates me or not is her choice. Not yours. Not mine. And if she doesn't believe I'm the man for her, I'll respect that. But don't threaten me. Don't ever threaten me again."

The newly arrived Luke followed Gio into the penthouse and gave Julia a kiss on the cheek. "Gio called and said Nick was looking a little ragged around the edges." Luke looked Nick over and whistled, "He was right. Now he says you're making breakfast? Mind if I join you?"

Once they were all seated around the kitchen table, Nick shared what Rena had told him about their mother and reiterated the threat she'd made to expose them. Nick slammed his hand down on the table beside his plate. "I've been thinking about it all night, and I can't figure out a way to stop her. She won't listen to any of us."

"We can't kill her," Gio joked darkly. When Julia kicked him beneath the table, Gio said, "I said *can't*."

Julia rested her chin on her hands and said wistfully, "It's too bad you don't have anything you could threaten to expose her for."

All three men looked at her in surprise and Julia shrugged. "I'm nice, but I'm not that nice. Your mother is bringing this on herself. I'll turn my cheek. I may even turn a second cheek. But if you threaten someone I love, you're going down."

Kane, who was finally beginning to relax, said, "Gio, marry this one fast."

Gio took one of Julia's hands in his and brought it to his lips. "I intend to." Then he turned to Nick. "Trust me, if I knew of something I'd use it. I threatened to cut her out of my life, and she escalated instead of backing off."

Luke sighed. "I would usually encourage open dialogue as a way to resolve an issue, but with what I'm learning about our mother, she won't care what any of us say. You can't reason with someone who has left all reason behind."

Nick thought back to something Rena had told him. "We don't have anything on Mother, but we may know someone who does."

Gio raised an eyebrow.

Nick said, "Rena said Uncle Alessandro warned Maddy to stay away from our mother. Rena said Aunt Elise suggested it was time Alessandro told us something. That something could be what we need."

Gio nodded. "It might be. They've known each other a long time."

Kane added, "I'll see if I can find out how she got pictures of Nick and Rena in the first place. She had to have hired someone. Maybe we can cut her off there."

Luke shook his head. "Did you ever think when we finally grew closer it would be over something like this?"

Nick drawled, "A family who plots together stays together."

Kane shook his head and the corner of his mouth twitched.

Nick shook a finger at him. "See, you're starting to get my sense of humor."

Kane opened his mouth to say something, but Julia interrupted, "More coffee anyone?"

Gio took a gulp out of his cup, then said, "I'll go see Alessandro tomorrow."

"No," Nick said firmly. "I will. Rena is my..." He stopped when he realized that she wasn't his anything. Not anymore. "Responsibility. I'll handle this."

Chapter Seventeen

RENA HAD JUST walked by Nick's office for the third time Monday morning when she finally broke down and opened the outer door. Janet was sitting at her desk, typing on her computer.

"Is Nick in?" Rena asked.

"No, he's out of the office this morning," Janet said, then looked up. "Oh, hi Rena. Yeah, Nick's not here."

Rena hovered beside the young woman's desk. "Is he actually not here, or did he tell you to say that if I asked?"

Janet grimaced with sympathy. "He's not in there. Are you okay? You look upset. Did you two have an argument? Tell me you didn't break up."

Rena pulled back in surprise. "No. No. We couldn't break up because Nick and I have never been together."

Janet rolled her eyes. "Okay, sure."

Rena knew she should leave, but curiosity kept her there. "Why, did he say anything to you? About me? About us? Not that there was anything to say because—"

Janet waved one hand in the air for comical emphasis. "It's okay. He didn't say anything. He didn't have to. The two of you are pretty obvious. You come here to moon over him. He goes up there to moon over you."

Rena blushed. She thought she was more sophisticated than that, but apparently she wasn't. "Well, thanks anyway."

"Did you want to leave him a message?" Janet asked.

"No." *God, no.* Rena thought. *I don't even know what to say when I see him. What would I put on a Post-it Note?* "I'm sure I'll see him around."

"Rena," Janet called out.

Rena turned at the door.

"I didn't know what to think of Nick when I first met him. He has quite a reputation, you know? But underneath all that, he's a good guy. Don't give up on him too easily." Janet ended her pep talk with a wink.

Rena spun around and walked into the doorjamb. She stumbled back and made a hasty second retreat. Once around the corner she leaned against the wall and caught her breath.

The idea that Janet was cheering them on from the sidelines shook Rena. Janet thought their relationship was real. Which made her face the ugly realization that Nick might have thought the same thing.

Rena couldn't breathe each time she entertained the possibility that Nick might have feelings for her. Nor could she breathe when she asked herself how she felt about him.

Love and suffocation—who knew they could feel so similar?

Rena covered her face and repeated the scary realization to herself. *I love Nick. I should have told him that when he came to me, upset and confused. I know his family well enough to know how bad that day was for him. But I was so afraid of admitting how I felt—even to myself—that I wasn't there for him when he most needed me.*

What kind of love is that?

Pushing off the wall, Rena headed back toward her office. If she truly had ruined her chance of being with Nick, her time at Cogent was over. Every window reminded her of a time they'd stopped beside it to tell each other about their days. She couldn't look at the elevator outside her office without thinking about the first time Nick had kissed her.

Rena sat at her desk and stared at her computer monitor without turning it on. She refused to start crying again. She thought back to how concerned her mother had looked when she'd rushed into her house on Saturday. Rena had cried and cried in her mother's arms until she had no tears left to shed.

She'd tried to explain, both to Kane and her mother, that she wasn't upset with Nick; she was disappointed in herself. She'd always blamed others for holding her back from doing what she really wanted to do. She'd had this fantasy version of herself she'd clung to for years, telling herself if she had a chance she would be bolder, braver.

In the end, she hadn't even been a good friend to Nick, and that was what she regretted the most. She'd told his brothers to have faith in him, but she hadn't. She would never forget the look in Nick's eyes when he'd walked away from her. Once again he'd been made to feel he wasn't good enough, and this time it was her fault.

Kane had been furious with Nick at first but then, surprisingly, he'd promised to remain neutral. Rena guessed it was because he feared if he didn't say so Rena was going to start crying all over him.

"Rena."

She looked up quickly at Gio's face, then cursed when she realized her cheeks were wet with tears. Angrily, she wiped them away. "Sorry," Rena said as she fumbled to find a tissue in her desk drawer. "Allergies."

"Come into my office."

"Sure," Rena said and followed him. She took a seat in one of the chairs before his desk, expecting him to sit behind it as he normally did. Instead, he paced back and forth beside it. Rena braced herself in anticipation of another lecture on why she and Nick didn't belong together. Gio continued not to say anything until Rena couldn't hold back her thoughts anymore. She burst out, "Gio, I know what you're going to say. You're angry because you found out Nick and I have been seeing each other and lying about it. You're probably going to tell me you don't think I should work here anymore, but before you do that, there is something I need to say." Tears misted up in her eyes, but she blinked them back. "Nick is an amazing man. He's honest. He's funny. He never did a single thing wrong with me. In fact, he was better to me than I was to him. So if you're going to be angry with anyone for this, I want to make sure you're upset with the right person. Me. Nick wanted to tell you about us, but I convinced him to keep it a secret. He didn't let you down, I did. You have your brother in your life again. Don't let something I did take that away from either of you."

Gio's face tightened. "Is the Lyndon report complete? I gave it to you on Thursday."

"Oh," Rena said and choked in surprise at his question. "Almost. I was adding your final notes from Friday."

"I need it finished by noon."

Rena stood. "I'll get right on it."

"Your personal life doesn't belong at work, Rena."

Well, that's a slap in the face if I ever felt one. "I understand, Gio."

Gio walked around his desk and sat down. He sorted through the mail on his desk while he spoke. "Now, if you want to have dinner with Julia and me on Thursday night, we could make sure Nick joins us."

Rena swayed where she stood. "Did you just say what I think you said?"

Gio looked up from the mail. "My brother would be one lucky son of a bitch if he ended up with you, and our family needs all the sanity we can marry into. I was wrong to tell either of you who you could be with. Let's leave it at that."

Rena rushed around Gio's desk, threw her arms around him, and burst into happy tears. "Thank you. Nick and I need to figure this out on our own, though. I don't think surprising him at dinner would help."

He awkwardly gave her a pat on the back and said, "You know what would help, Rena? Work. I need that report."

Rena stepped back and laughed, drying her eyes on her sleeve. "Yes, sir."

"And, Rena, it'll go a lot faster if you turn your computer on."

ଔ

Nick sat on the stone railing of his uncle's patio and looked out over acres of manicured lawn. He'd traveled halfway around the world to attend an Andrade wedding, but this was Nick's first time at the Andrade family home in New York. He marveled at the blend of old-world wealth and modern-day tricycles. The area closet to the enormous home was dotted with gym sets and sandboxes.

Alessandro stood a few feet away, gazing out over his land along with Nick. "It's beautiful, isn't it? Elise and I wanted our piece of the American dream, and this is where we found it. You came on a quiet day. Every Sunday that lawn is full of generations of Andrades. Maddy's husband is a world-renowned French chef, but on Sundays he cooks Italian for us. Do you remember all those cousins you met on Isola Santos? Half of them live around here. You should come by and get to know them."

"I may take you up on that offer."

"You're always welcome here, Nick. You always were."

Nick met his uncle's eyes and saw only sincerity there. "Do you know my father's second family in Venice?"

A sadness entered Alessandro's eyes. "I know of them."

"I knew about them long before I had proof. Even when my father was with us, part of him was somewhere else. That's why I was the daredevil I was. He said he worried for me. I suppose I thought if I gave him enough to worry about he wouldn't forget me when he went away."

Shaking his head sadly, Alessandro said, "Your father loved you."

"My father didn't know what love was. He said he loved my mother, but you tell me what kind of love allows a man to lie to his family as much as he lied to ours?"

Alessandro walked over and laid a hand on Nick's shoulder. "Love is a funny thing. It can bring out the best and the worst in people. I don't agree with what your father did, but that doesn't change how much I miss him. It's okay to be angry with him, but it's not okay to use him as an excuse to be less than the man you should be."

Nick whipped his shoulder away from Alessandro's hand. "What do you mean, less than I should be?"

In an authoritative tone, Alessandro said, "I don't agree with how you're treating little Rena. I met her. You should give her more respect and not hide what you're doing. She deserves more than what you're giving her."

Nick folded his arms across his chest. "I'm not giving her anything anymore. We're not together."

Alessandro sighed. "That's a shame. I really liked her."

Nick turned back toward his uncle and said, "I do, too. In fact, I fell in love with her, but that's not why I'm here. We need your help."

With a bold wave of his hands, Alessandro said, "Anything. What do you need?"

"My mother has threatened to share certain photos of Rena and me in compromising situations. There is nothing I can say to stop my mother, but I'm hoping there is something you can."

Shaking his head, his uncle stepped back. "I haven't spoken to your mother in years."

Nick advanced and said, "But you knew her well when she was younger, didn't you? There has to be something she doesn't want people to know about her. I used to go crazy asking myself why my mother was the way she was. I don't care anymore. All I care about is protecting Rena from her. If you know something, Alessandro, you have to tell me."

Alessandro leaned back against the stone railing and seemed to be weighing something in his mind. Finally he said, "What happened to your mother is not my story to tell, but I will speak to her. You're right. There are things Patrice doesn't want anyone to know and it's time she discovers that someone does. Tell Rena she'll have nothing to worry about when it comes to Patrice. I should have stepped forward and confronted Patrice years ago, but I had no idea how dark her heart had become."

Nick grabbed his uncle's arm. "You're honestly not going to tell me?"

Alessandro laid his hand over Nick's. "There are truths that bring families closer together, and there are others with the potential to tear them apart. This is one that finally needs to be put to rest—but not before it stops your mother. I promise you that."

Before Nick had a chance to ask another question, his aunt joined them. "So this is where the two of you are hiding. Are you hungry, Nick?"

Chapter Eighteen

BEFORE HEADING BACK to work, Nick stopped at Skal. It wasn't open yet, but he merely had to say four-one-one to the man guarding the door to be let in. It was Serge's little joke. Four-one-one meant: For your information, I'm someone you open the door for without question.

He found Serge behind the bar counting bottles.

Serge saw Nick and exclaimed, "Where the hell have you been? I've missed you."

Nick sat down at the bar and accepted the club soda Serge poured him. "Working."

"So, how is being a big businessman? Better than the party life?"

Nick swirled his drink and considered both before answering. "You know, I won't lie to you, being wild and carefree was definitely easier. But I feel good about what I'm doing, and happy—even though half the time I don't know if I'm doing any of it well."

"You'll get there, Nicky. Should I ask about... you know who?"

Nick took a drink of his soda. "You were right and you were wrong, Serge. I did end up wanting the house and kids. Ridiculous, right? Me? What I didn't count on was, when you've built up a reputation for not taking love seriously, it tends not to take you seriously back."

Serge put a bowl of nuts in front of Nick. "There will be other women, Nick. There always are."

Nick picked up a nut, tossed it in the air, and caught it. "I don't think so, Serge. This was the one."

"Did you sleep with her sister?"

Nick laid the nut down on the bar in front of him. "She doesn't have a sister."

"You know what I mean."

"No, I was completely faithful." Nick pushed the rest of the nuts away. "I'm not even attracted to other women anymore. I mean, I still know they're beautiful, but there's only one woman I want to be with." He spun the peanut before him.

"Have you tried telling her that?"

Nick slammed his hand down on the nut. "Words mean nothing, Serge. People lie every day. I could buy her flowers and talk her back into my bed, but I want more than that. I want her to believe in me. And she doesn't. Words can't change that."

"You really love this woman?"

"I do."

Serge picked up a handful of nuts. "Then you need to believe in her, too." He popped the snacks in his mouth. "She'll come around."

Nick looked up and smiled. "That's pretty optimistic for a jaded old coot."

Serge shrugged. "Get back to that office of yours. I've got a business to run."

Nick stood. "Thanks, Serge."

Serge picked up Nick's glass and wiped a cloth over where it had sat. "Whatever. Go on, get out of here."

Nick paused outside the building to look at it in the harsh light of the day. He'd gone there for more years than he could remember. Once he would have said it was the quality of the music and the free-flowing booze that kept him going back.

Amazing that neither had been there during this visit, and it hadn't made one damn difference to how good he felt when he left. He didn't want to return to the life he'd once lived, but it was nice to know that some of his friendships from that time would remain.

Right there on the sidewalk, he rang his mother.

"Hello?"

"Hello, Mother."

"Nick, I was hoping you'd call. I've missed you."

A wondrous feeling washed over Nick. He wasn't confused anymore. "Mother, I want you to know that Alessandro Andrade will be coming to see you. I sent him."

"I don't understand what you're talking about, Nick. Why would you send your uncle here when you know how badly he's always treated me?"

"He's coming to give you a chance, Mother, your last chance to stop. I know what you said to Rena."

His mother sputtered, then said, "I don't know what lies that woman told you..."

"It's over, Mother. We see you for who you are. All you have left is whatever goddamn secret Alessandro respects you too much to tell us. But if one photo of Rena leaks out, if I hear that you called her or even said her name, I will not stop until I expose you and that secret to the world."

"Nick, you need me. Who is going to look out for you? You think your brothers will?"

"I know they will. You know why? Because they're Andrades, and to an Andrade, family is everything."

"You can say that to me? Nick? Your mother? Even while you're threatening me?"

"I can. You're a Stanfield. You always have been. You never wanted to be one of us. Now you won't be."

"I am half of who you are, Nick."

"Yes, Mother, and that's exactly why you should be afraid of me. Don't call me again. We're done."

ﻉ

It was late afternoon when Rena rounded a corner at Cogent and walked straight into Nick. He steadied her with a hand on either arm, then released her. "Sorry," he said.

Everything Rena had planned to say to him flew out of her head. She studied his face. He looked tired. She wanted to ask him why, but she wasn't sure how. There was so much she felt she had to say before that. "Nick."

"Yes?"

"I—"

A man from marketing walked by, stopped, and asked, "Mr. Andrade. I wanted to thank you for giving me credit for the social media campaign idea I had for Easton. It landed me a promotion."

Nick clapped a hand on the man's back. "You came up with the idea, Ben. I'm glad it worked out for you."

The man shook Nick's hand. "Anytime you need anything, I'm right downstairs. I even have an office now."

Nick nodded. "I'll make sure to drop by."

After the man had left, Rena couldn't help but say, "Looks like you're building a loyal following here."

Nick shrugged and leaned in. "He told me his idea while we were in the men's room a few weeks ago. Thankfully, it was while we were washing our hands. He was a nervous wreck, but what he said made sense. We had been trying to break into the Easton area, and public opinion about our project improved after we made the campaign more personal. It was a good idea."

Rena froze. The feel of Nick's breath on her ear sent her thoughts scattering again. She wanted to turn her head and kiss him with all the emotions swirling within her. She dropped the folder she was holding, causing its contents to scatter across the floor.

Nick bent and began to gather them. She did the same. The two of them almost knocked heads as they reached for the same paper.

"Thank you," Rena said as she stuffed everything back in the folder.

Nick held her eyes as if waiting for her to say something. *Should I start with an apology?* she asked herself in a wild panic. *Tell him I missed him? Beg him to forgive me?*

"You don't have to worry anymore about the photos of us coming out. That problem has been dealt with."

Rena rushed to reassure him. "Thank you." *Oh, my God.* Rena chastised herself. *That's the best I can do? All I'm going to say?* "Nick—"

Nick waited.

Another coworker stopped to ask if Nick had seen the specs he'd sent and if they were what he'd wanted. Nick told him they were on his desk and that he'd email him before the end of the day. The man walked away, and Rena decided the office was not the place for what she had to say.

Before she lost her nerve, she blurted out. "Nick, would you go out with me tonight?"

Nick's expression didn't reveal his thoughts. "It's Monday."

Rena's eyes misted up, but she sniffed back the tears angrily. "There's a movie playing I've wanted to see. I'd really like to see it with you."

"Are you asking me out on a date, Rena?"

Rena smiled and sniffed again. "I am."

"You know what dates lead to? Actual relationships."

Clasping her cold hands in front of her, Rena said, "That's what I'm hoping."

After a long moment, Nick said, "Okay. I'll see you tonight." He leaned forward like he was going to kiss her, then stopped, and with his lips hovering just above hers he asked, "Where do you want to meet?"

"At my house?" Rena asked breathily.

A slow grin spread across Nick's face as he straightened. "Maybe we should meet at the theater. It's not good to put out on the first date."

Rena laughed in surprise and swatted at him. Her heart was pounding so hard in her chest she wondered if he could hear it. She said, "You're such a jerk," but she was still laughing as she said it.

Nick feigned a serious expression and said, "I don't want you to think I'm easy. I want you to respect me."

Rena's laughter fell away, and she heard the question behind his joke. "I do, Nick. More than you'll ever know. I was scared, and I was wrong."

Nick pulled her to him for a passionate kiss that left them both shaking and clinging to each other. He hugged her to his chest, and Rena heard his heart beating as wildly as her own.

With his usual dry humor, he said, "I'm sure I'll think of a way for you to make it up to me." Then he kissed her briefly one last time and walked away.

Rena floated back to her office in a warm daze. Everything that had seemed so hopeless earlier now felt possible.

She sat at her desk and dreamily rested her chin on her hands.

Gio picked up the folder in front of her and said, "I'll finish the Lyndon report, Rena. Don't strain yourself."

Rena waved at him wordlessly. Her body was still at work, but the rest of her was halfway home, deciding what to wear on her first date with Nick.

Chapter Nineteen

THE FOLLOWING SATURDAY afternoon, Rena paced in her living room as she waited for Nick. He hadn't told her where they were going so she'd changed three times already, finally settling on a simple sleeveless blue dress. She didn't know what to expect. The past week had been wonderful and confusing.

Monday night they had snuggled at the movie theater, eaten their weight in popcorn, and whispered to each other enough to annoy the people around them. Afterward, they had held hands and walked the High Line through Chelsea. They'd caught a cab, and Rena had blissfully snuggled against him the whole ride back to her house. He'd given her a passionate good night kiss and, much to Rena's shock, left her at the door.

On Tuesday, he'd sent her one red rose and a note asking her to meet him for lunch. They'd skirted off together to a local art museum, where they'd spent an hour pretending they knew more about the paintings than they did, and calling bullshit each time they caught each other spouting blatant fiction. They had laughed so hard their sides hurt and others had shushed them, which had only made them laugh harder.

Early Wednesday, Nick had met her at Central Park and they'd gone for a jog together. They'd raced to landmarks, chased a few pigeons, and lay in each other's arms, talking, before each heading back home to change for work. They'd both been late to Cogent that day, but no one had said a thing.

On Thursday they had laughed their way through the realization that there was nothing romantic about the pottery class Nick had chosen for their date. Their very strict instructor had chastised them for trying to use the same pottery wheel, and although they had both talked a good game, neither had successfully created anything but a mess. It didn't matter, though. Nothing mattered to Rena besides the joy of being with Nick. That night, just as he had on Monday, Nick had kissed her soundly and had left her on her doorstep completely confused.

By Friday, Rena couldn't imagine being happier. She and Nick had found a small restaurant in SoHo where they'd eaten off each other's plates and talked until the restaurant closed. By the time Nick had walked her to her door, it had been one in the morning.

Saturday morning.

Rena had been positive he'd come inside with her. After all, Saturday had always been their special day. She'd been disappointed when she'd opened her door and he'd made no move to follow her inside. It hadn't made sense to her. They'd never been happier together. Rena had asked him if he wanted to come in, but he'd said he'd be back that afternoon. He had a surprise for her.

When he came to the door, pulling her out of her reverie, he was, surprisingly, dressed in a suit, Rena felt glad she'd chosen a dress suitable for many situations. He'd also brought along a driver for his town car.

"Where are we going?" Rena asked when she settled into the backseat beside Nick.

"Home," he said vaguely, then silenced her next question with a kiss.

Their car headed over the Brooklyn Bridge. Rena watched the city disappear behind them and was filled with curiosity. "Did you buy a house, Nick?"

He gave her an infuriatingly vague look. "You'll just have to wait and see, won't you? I'll give you a hint—it's not a hot air balloon ride."

Rena smiled. "Hey, that turned out well."

He tucked her into his side and kissed her forehead. "I remember."

Rena leaned back so she could see his face. "Just tell me if this is the kind of Saturday we used to have, or a date like the kind we've been going on all week."

Her question gained her a lopsided grin in response. "Which would you rather have?"

Rena ran a hand along Nick's thigh and squeezed it. "Do I have to choose? They were all amazing."

He laid his hand on hers, then brought her hand to his lips. "I agree."

Rena turned his face toward hers. "You're not going to even give me a hint?"

"I did. Home."

Rena sighed. "You're killing me."

Their car pulled over to a small park on the beach. The driver handed Nick a blanket and a small basket. It was a cool early-autumn evening and the beach was deserted. Nick led her to the edge of the water and laid the blanket down. Rena shivered and Nick took off his jacket, placing it around her shoulders before they both settled on the blanket.

Rena joked, "We're a little overdressed for a day at the beach."

Nick took one of her hands in his and said, "I thought of a hundred different ways to do this. Some of them included jetting you off to Europe. I even started to research one here in the city, I was going to pay off the night guard at the Natural Museum of Science, and he was going to let us have a few hours alone in the woolly mammoth display case. I pictured a sort of caveman-cavewoman theme."

"What are you talking about?"

Nick looked out of the ocean and said, "Don't rush me. I'm nervous."

Rena's breath caught in her throat. Nick wasn't the nervous type. She squeezed his hand and waited, even though she thought she might pass out from the anticipation building inside her. He couldn't be about to ask what she thought he was, could he? "Why are you nervous?"

He turned toward her and took both of her hands in his. "This is important. I don't want any more misunderstandings. I didn't come from a family like yours, Rena." He stopped and looked down in frustration. "I probably don't have to explain that to you. You know my family."

Rena gave his hands a squeeze and said, "It's just me. You don't have to choose your words carefully. Just say it."

He looked up and met her eyes. "I've been looking for something my whole life. I didn't know what it was, but I do now. I want a home, Rena. Not a big empty house where people live but don't actually talk to each other. I want somewhere full of love and laughter. A place where I can be myself and know I belong. And that's what you are to me, Rena. You're home to me."

Tears welled up in Rena's eyes and started running down her cheeks. She would have wiped them away but Nick was still holding her hands. "You're home to me, too, Nick. When I'm with you I feel like I can finally be myself. Like I'm finally free."

"I love you, Rena. Say you'll marry me, and I'll spend the rest of my life proving to you why this is the right choice."

Although Rena was tempted to simply throw her arms around him and chant yes a hundred times, she felt a playfulness when she was with Nick that she could not suppress. She looked up at him from beneath her long lashes and asked, "Will we still have our Saturday dates? Because I've never had sex with a caveman."

Nick hauled her to him and rained kisses on her face. "Oh, you just wait and see where I take you next time."

Rena gave him a saucy smile. "I have a few ideas of my own." She kissed him deeply, then said, "I love you, Nick Andrade. I will marry you today, tomorrow, wherever, or whenever you want. I don't care. As long as we're together."

Nick reached into his pocket and pulled out a box. When he opened it, Rena recognized the simple diamond solitaire inside and gasped. Nick said, "Your mother said this was her mother's ring. She said your grandparents were married for fifty years so it has to be full of a lot of love. If you want a new one, I'll buy you one, but I thought..."

Rena slid the ring on, then went up onto her knees and kissed Nick again. "No, this is perfect." Then she stopped as a thought came to her. "How did you get this ring? Did you go see my parents? Did you tell them you were going to ask me to marry you?"

Nick nodded and grinned.

Rena looked down at the ring in shock. "How did that go?"

"We sorted a few things out, but in the end we agreed the most important thing in all this was your happiness. And I can make you happy, Rena. I know I can."

Rena kissed him, then hugged him tightly. "You already do."

CR

A short time later, when Nick and Rena were back in the car, Nick sent a text: **We're on our way.**

Rena peered over and asked, "You're texting someone now?"

Nick wrapped an arm around her and pulled her close. "Your mother wanted to make sure everything was ready when we arrived."

"My mother?"

Nick smiled. "You have one more surprise today. I hope it's what you wanted. I think it is."

Even though Rena tried to pry hints out of him, Nick refused to say more on the long drive. The street leading to her parents' driveway was lined with cars. Rena sat up and craned her neck so she could see better as they approached. "Are my parents having a party?"

Nick kissed her shoulder. "Technically we are, but they're hosting it."

Rena looked back at him, her eyes round with wonder. "An engagement party?"

"Yes."

"That's a bold move. What if I had said no?"

He pulled her back against him and buried his face in her neck. "I didn't let myself consider that possibility."

They pulled up to the front of the house and Rena gripped Nick's arms as she looked around. "Nick, there has to be a hundred people here. Who did you invite?"

He took her hand and led her toward the house. "I started with your family, then my brothers, and some of my friends I'd like you to meet. Then I called Uncle Alessandro and asked him if there were any Andrades around who wanted to come celebrate our engagement. Apparently there are a lot of them."

A pack of children ran past them like a stampeding herd. Rena laughed. "Do you know all of them?"

Nick pointed to a man who ran past after the children. "That's my second cousin Tino." Another man called for the first man to get his child back in the yard too. "Or that's Tino. I'm still learning all their names." He put a hand on Rena's back and guided her closer. "I'm hoping you can help me sort them out."

Rena shook her head in amazement at the number of family who had come out to support Nick and said, "It might take a while."

Nick leaned down and kissed the tip of her nose. "That's okay, we have a lifetime together to figure it out."

Epilogue

TWO WEEKS LATER, Rena had a cab drop her off in front of the impressive Corisi home where Maddy had requested her presence for what she said was an important family meeting.

Keep your friends close, and your wacky family members closer, Rena thought. With someone like Maddy, it wasn't a bad idea to attend her meetings just to keep abreast of what she was up to.

Abby Corisi opened the front door of her home and graciously welcomed Rena with a warm hug, beckoning her to enter. Nicole Andrade, Nick's cousin through marriage, rushed over to also hug Rena.

Maddy joined them with a cautious smile. "Thanks for coming, Rena. I wasn't sure if you would." The sad eyes she gave Rena reminded her of the momentary contrition of a puppy who had been caught shredding something and would soon be off to shred something else. It was a clear act of manipulation, but one that was impossible to resist. Maddy's father had hit the reason dead on the head when he'd said his daughter was all heart. She might be impulsive and have a penchant for meddling, but she meant well.

Rena reluctantly smiled. "I'm not angry with you anymore, Maddy."

Maddy threw her arms around Rena and gave her a bone-crushing hug. "I never meant to hurt you, Rena. I can't tell you how sorry I am."

Rena hugged her back. "I realize you didn't know what Patrice was capable of."

Abby requested they follow her into one of the house's side salons. As they walked, Maddy linked arms with Rena and said, "She can't be as awful as you think she is. She's Nick's mother and my aunt. Sometimes people go through things that give them a bitter outer shell, but everyone has good in them."

Rena pulled Maddy to a halt and bore into her with her eyes. "It's nice to be optimistic about people, Maddy, but not when it endangers the ones you love. Don't trust Patrice. She has very few allies right now and if she can use you, she will. I may not be related to her, but I've seen her up close and in action for a long time. You don't know who you're dealing with."

Maddy let Rena's arm drop. "I'm not an idiot, you know. But I also don't write people off just because they've made some mistakes."

Nicole touched Maddy's arm gently. "I don't think you're an idiot, Maddy. You've lived a blessed life where you've never had to deal with anyone like Patrice. My father was an angry and vindictive man. I regret not cutting my father out of life. It took his death for me to admit what he'd put my family through. Be careful with your aunt. Stephan says she's an unhappy woman who seems hell-bent on sabotaging her own sons. Listen to what Rena is saying. She's speaking from a loving place, too."

With uncharacteristically sad eyes, Maddy asked, "So, what are you suggesting, that I ignore her when she calls? That I stop going to see her?"

"Yes," Rena and Nicole said in unison.

"I don't know if I can do that," Maddy said seriously.

Their talk was cut off as they entered a room full of other women. Julia put down the cup of tea she was sipping when she saw Rena and patted the open space next to her on the couch. She joked, "Yay, now I'm not the only newbie here."

Nicole stepped closer to Rena. "They will appear crazy at first, but you'll never meet a more supportive or genuinely loving group of women. I married into some of this, but all of them are family now."

Abby smiled warmly at Nicole. "I don't remember life before all of you. I don't want to."

A beautiful woman with similar but leaner features and an easy smile walked over and put her arm around Abby's shoulders. "It was just you and me."

A tall, stunning redhead flipped her hair over one shoulder and said, "Don't forget me, Lil. I was right there with you, driving Abby nuts."

Abby waved a finger playfully at the redhead. "You certainly were, Alethea. Someday you'll have children and I will enjoy watching them put you through your paces."

Alethea smiled unabashedly at Abby. "Marc will keep them in line."

Nicole laughed. "Rena, as you probably know, Abby is married to my brother, Dominic. Her sister, Lil, is married to Jake Walton, Dominic's business partner. Alethea is Lil's best friend. Never lie to her, she's on Dominic's security force and probably already knows your bank account balance to the penny. It's a little scary, but you'll get used to her. The woman sitting in the chair beside Julia is Marie Duhamel. She'll tell you she's my brother's personal assistant, but really she's like a den mother around here and a genius when it comes to solving problems. Keep her number handy. I don't know how she does it. Sometimes I think she has a magic wand she won't tell us about. Either way, if you need anything, she's the one to call. I believe you know that I'm a first cousin to Maddy through my husband, Stephan. And, of course, you already know Julia."

"Wow," Rena said with a chuckle. "I'll try to remember everyone's name. Please be patient with me—I've met a lot of people recently."

Abby took a seat beside Marie. "Marie, I told you about that, right? Nick called Maddy's father and asked if there were any Andrades who wanted to attend an engagement party."

The very properly dressed older woman slapped her lap and laughed. "He didn't."

Maddy and Nicole sat down across from them. "He did," Maddy said with a huge smile.

Alethea and Lil sat together on the end of a chaise lounge. Alethea shook her head at the group in amusement. "No one thought to warn him?"

Lil leaned against her friend in camaraderie. "Now where would the fun be in that?"

While Nicole poured herself a cup of tea, she said, "It's funny, but it's also heartwarming to see Nick reaching out to the family the way he is. Stephan's father called and there was no option except going, but we didn't mind. Not a day goes by that I don't thank the powers above for bringing all of you into my life."

Marie dabbed at her eyes with a napkin. "Don't, Nicole. I don't want to start bawling and ruin my makeup."

Maddy uncrossed her legs and leaned forward. "See, this is why I called a meeting. Family doesn't just happen. It's a choice we make. Uncle Victor understands that. Many families stop gathering because it's inconvenient or because someone is arguing with someone. Yes, we argue, but Andrades don't give up on each other. We're so close to our goal. We can't stop now."

Rena looked across at Julia. She mouthed silently, "This is a meeting? What goal?"

Julia shrugged her shoulders and shook her head.

With sudden insight, Rena asked, "Is this about the bet you all have going about who is the best matchmaker?"

"It's more than a bet," Maddy said earnestly. "And it's already working. Julia, since you met Gio, he's spending more time with his brothers, isn't he?"

Julia nodded, but she didn't look comfortable agreeing.

Maddy turned to Rena. "And look at what happened when you and Nick got together. That was the first time one of George's sons invited the rest of the family to one of their events. You did that, Rena."

Rena shook her head. "Technically, Nick did."

"Because being with you made him see how important family is," Maddy countered. She looked around the room and stared down each woman one at a time. "Is there anyone here who doesn't agree with that? Hasn't the love that has come into your life brought each of you to a better place?"

Abby glanced at Marie. "I am always most afraid when I find myself agreeing with Maddy. I want to tell her to stop, but her track record is irrefutable."

Alethea tapped her long nails on the side of the cup she was holding. "I have to disagree. Julia wasn't one of our plants. She met Gio on her own. Rena has known Nick for most of her life. We're not responsible for any of this."

Maddy rolled her eyes. "Alethea, you can sit there and toss your facts around—"

Alethea raised one of her perfectly groomed eyebrows. "It's called reality."

Lil gave Alethea's leg a pat. "Remember the filter we talked about?"

Abby started laughing so hard she had to wipe her eyes. "Lil, are you honestly lecturing Alethea about filtering what she says? I'm sorry, that is the funniest thing I've ever heard. Do you hear yourself?"

Marie sighed. "Ladies, we're not here to discuss us. Maddy is trying to make a point."

Nicole looked across at Rena and Julia. "They bicker like this all the time, it's harmless."

Maddy smoothed her dress over her legs and cleared her throat. "As I was saying, regardless of how it is happening, we are trying to bring the family back together by finding wives for my cousins and it's working. Do you disagree, Alethea?"

Alethea waved a hand in concession. "I concede that point."

"And as new members of the family, Julia and Rena, I thought you should join one of our teams," Maddy added.

"Teams?" Rena asked. She was starting to doubt that this conversation was real; in fact, she half expected that at any moment one of them would break down and admit it was all a prank.

Lil smiled at Alethea. "Al and I are a team."

Abby hugged Marie. "I snagged Marie."

Maddy took Nicole's hand in hers and raised it up triumphantly. "Nicole and I are a team and, being Andrades ourselves, we have inside information."

Lil blurted out, "Probably not as much as Alethea has."

Abby frowned at her sister. "Please tell me you're not using Jeremy for any of this."

Lil shrugged. "Not use Jeremy? That's like asking Superman not to fly. You can't start making up rules now, Abby."

Julia placed her cup down on the table in front of her. "Who is Jeremy?"

Marie said, "A wonderful, talented man who should be allowed to enjoy his time out in California with Jeisa."

Alethea sat up straighter and narrowed her eyes. "If I hadn't involved him last time, we wouldn't be here discussing the love lives of two grown men as if we actually have some control over them. We wouldn't care about any of this."

Abby shuddered. "You're right, Alethea. We're all grateful for what you do, it's just scary sometimes what you're able to uncover."

"Some secrets add to your life. Like finding out about Gigi. I want to invite her to spend Christmas with us. What do you think?"

Nicole asked, "Have you met her yet?"

"No," Maddy said cheerfully. "But she'll love us once she meets us."

Julia grimaced. "I don't know if that's a good idea. Gio is in contact with her now and it's a little rocky."

"See, secrets make things worse instead of better." Maddy cocked her head to one side and said, "My father said there is a reason Aunt Patrice is as bitter as she is. He won't tell me. Would you be able to find out, Alethea? Are you that good?"

"Oh, she is"—Lil said emphatically, then changed course when her sister glared at her from across the room—"not able to get involved in anything like that anymore."

In a kind tone, Marie interjected, "Maddy, there may be a very good reason your father doesn't want you to know. Some things are better left in the past."

Looking up at the ceiling with impatience, Maddy said, "You can't have it both ways. You can't tell me that I don't know someone well enough to know how to behave around her and also that I shouldn't try to learn more about her. I want to know what happened between Patrice and my family. It kept my cousins away from me. I want the truth." She turned to Alethea. "If you can uncover it, please help me."

Alethea looked around the room, studying the expressions of the women who watched her closely. Finally, she said sadly, "I keep my investigations purely business related now."

Maddy gave a delicate snort of disbelief. "So, you haven't been looking into the Andrades as part of this game? Is Lil wrong?"

Alethea didn't say anything.

Maddy pushed, "Yes or no, Alethea? Are you a hypocrite or a liar?"

Alethea stood, her temper also rising. "You don't know what you're asking me to do, Maddy. No one is ever grateful for what I uncover. They say they are, but people always blame the bearer of the bad news. I don't want to be that person anymore."

Maddy pursed her lips angrily. "So, you won't help me?"

Alethea looked down at Lil, then back at Maddy. "No, I won't. Sorry, Maddy."

An awkward silence fell over the room.

Marie moved to stand behind Maddy and laid a hand on her shoulder. "Maddy, tell us why you asked us here today. Didn't it have something to do with Max?"

Maddy crossed her arms across her chest and took a deep breath. She shook her head a few times in disappointment, then sighed and said, "Max didn't go to Rena and Nick's engagement party."

Rena said, "He's still out of the country."

Maddy countered, "He would have flown in if he'd wanted to. Julia, he said he might not come to your wedding, either." She sounded more than a little disheartened when she added, "I thought we should focus on him next. We have a few months. Are you planning it around Christmas?" She blinked quickly and tears filled her eyes when Julia didn't immediately answer. "Or maybe we should forget the bet. Maybe it's just another one of my stupid ideas."

Julia walked over and squished herself into the small space between Maddy and the arm of the couch. "We haven't picked a date yet. I admire what you're trying to do, Maddy, and I'd like to join your team, if you'll have me. I agree with Nicole, not a day goes by that I'm not grateful to have you and your family in my life. And if you think helping Max find love will bring him home, I'm in." She smiled across at Alethea. "It'll help even the odds, too. I was also in security."

Alethea choked and Lil elbowed her.

Rena stood. "Way to put my feet to the fire, Julia. I guess I'm in, too." She looked back and forth between the two remaining teams. Abby and Marie were definitely the saner choice, but there was a group that might need to be reined in. "I choose Lil and Alethea's team."

Lil let out a happy whoop. "You won't regret this. We may have had a slow start, but we're honing our skills. There are two brothers left. It's anyone's game."

Rena sat down next to Alethea.

Alethea looked her over and said, "It'll be interesting getting to know you."

Rena met her eyes squarely and smiled, "I was thinking exactly the same about you."

03

Later that day, Rena met Nick at the coffee shop near her house. The owners always gave them a strange look when they entered, but that was part of what made it fun to go there. The security officer at the Natural Museum of Science gave them that same look when they visited the prehistoric exhibit a week after their wild romp there.

Rena sipped her coffee and lovingly watched Nick tell her about a business call he'd received. He'd asked her how her day had gone with Maddy and the ladies, and she'd given him a vague answer. He was finally happy and she didn't want him worrying about his family again. She'd tell him everything, as soon as there was anything concrete to share.

Getting to know Nick's family was going to be a challenge, but Rena felt up to the task. She may not have agreed with how Maddy and the other ladies approached certain issues, but she didn't doubt they did what they did out of love.

Even Alethea, who gave off the vibe of being a shark in otherwise calm waters. Her obsession with delving into other people's private lives was confirmed by the stories the women had shared later that afternoon.

Luckily I have nothing to hide. Well, almost nothing. Rena smiled and imagined what Alethea would discover if she also dabbled in surveillance.

Hey, if she goes there—she deserves what she sees.

When Nick ended his story, Rena leaned over and whispered in his ear, "I've never been to a baseball game. We should go to one."

Nick's face transformed with a heart-melting, sexy grin, "During the week or on Saturday?"

Rena winked.

And Nick nodded.

Saturday it is.

The End

Can't wait to read the next book in The Andrades Series?

Go to RuthCardello.com and add your email to the mailing list.

We'll send you an email as soon as the next book is released!

Printed in Great Britain
by Amazon

45951655R00129